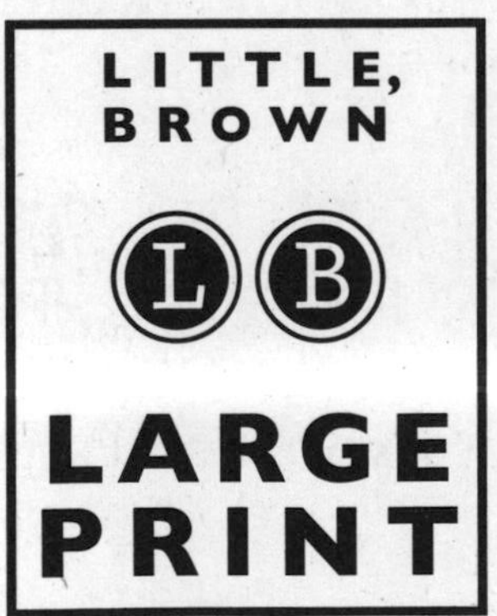
LITTLE,
BROWN
L B
LARGE
PRINT

BOOKS BY JAMES PATTERSON

FEATURING MICHAEL BENNETT

Worst Case (with Michael Ledwidge)

Run for Your Life (with Michael Ledwidge)

Step on a Crack (with Michael Ledwidge)

A complete list of books by James Patterson is on pages 405–407. For previews of upcoming books by James Patterson and more information about the author, visit www.JamesPatterson.com.

Worst Case

A NOVEL

James Patterson
AND
Michael Ledwidge

LITTLE, BROWN AND COMPANY

LARGE PRINT EDITION

Little, Brown and Company
Hachette Book Group
237 Park Avenue, New York, NY 10017
Visit our website at www.HachetteBookGroup.com

First Large Print Edition: February 2010

Little, Brown and Company is a division of Hachette Book Group, Inc. The Little, Brown name and logo are trademarks of Hachette Book Group, Inc.

ISBN 978-0-316-05570-3
LCCN 2009927754

10 9 8 7 6 5 4 3 2 1

RRD-IN

Printed in the United States of America

For Susan Maloney, Sue Najork,
Marlene Stang, and Kary Tangredi—J.P.

For Mary Ann O'Donnell, World's Greatest Adviser
Special thanks to "Uncle" Ed Kelly and
Judge Joe Len—M.L.

Prologue

GIVE PEACE A CHANCE . . . OR ELSE

One

THE STOCKY MAN with the salt-and-pepper hair felt light-headed as he crossed beneath the marble arch into Washington Square Park. He dropped his backpack, took off his circular glasses, and blotted the sudden tears in his eyes with the sleeve of his ancient jeans jacket.

He hadn't planned on breaking down, but My God, he thought, wiping at his rugged, lined face. Now he knew how Vietnam veterans felt when they visited their Wall down in Washington, DC. If veterans of the antiwar movement had a monument—a Wall of Tears—it was here, where it all began, Washington Square Park.

Staring out over the windy park, he remembered

all the incredible things that had occurred here. The antiwar demonstrations. Bob Dylan in the 4th Street basement clubs, singing about which way the wind was blowing. The candlelit faces of his old friends as they passed bottles and smoke. The whispered promises they had made to one another to change things, to make things better.

He looked out over the Friday-afternoon crowd by the center fountain, the people hovering over the chess tables, as if he might find a familiar face. But that was impossible, wasn't it? he thought with a shrug. They'd all moved on, like he had. Grown up. Sold out. Or were underground. Figuratively. Literally.

That time, *his* time, was almost completely faded now, just about dead and gone.

Just about, he thought as he knelt and removed the box of flyers from his knapsack.

But not quite.

On each of the five hundred sheets was a three-paragraph message entitled LOVE CAN CHANGE THE WORLD.

Who says you can't go home? he thought. A quote from Keith Richards popped into his head as he stacked the sheets.

"I got news for you. We're still a bunch of tough bastards. String us up and we still won't die."

You said it, Keith, he thought, giggling to himself. Right on, brother. You and me both.

More and more over the last year, his thoughts kept coming back to his youth. It was the only time in his entire life when he'd felt like he meant something, when he'd felt he was making a positive difference.

Was coming back now after all this time a midlife crisis? Maybe. He didn't care. He'd decided he wanted that feeling again. Especially in light of recent events. The world now was in even more dire straits than the one he and his friends had fought to affect. It was time to do it again. Wake people up before it was too late.

That's why he was here. It had worked once. They had, after all, stopped a war. Maybe it could happen again. Even if he was a lot older, he wasn't dead yet. Not by any means.

He licked his thumb and took the first sheet from the stack. He smiled, remembering the countless flyers he'd handed out in Berkeley and Seattle, and in Chicago in '68. After all this time, here he was. Unbelievable. What a crazy life. Back in the saddle again.

Two

"HI THERE," he said, offering the flyer to a young black woman pushing a toddler in a stroller.

He smiled at her, making eye contact. He was good with people, always had been. "I have a message here that I think you should take a look at, if it's not too much trouble. It concerns, well, everything."

"Leave me the hell alone with that nonsense," she said with surprising vehemence, almost smacking it out of his hand.

Had to expect a little of that, he thought with a nod. Some people were a hard sell. Came with the territory. Unfazed, he immediately walked over toward a group of teenagers skateboarding by the statue of Garibaldi.

"Afternoon, guys. I have a message here that I'd like you to read. Only take a second out of your day. If you're concerned about the state of affairs and about our future, I think it's something you should really consider."

They stared at him, dumbfounded. Up close, he was surprised to see the crow's-feet around their eyes. They weren't teenagers. They were in their late twenties and early thirties. Hard-looking. Kind of mean, actually.

"Holy shit! It's John Lennon!" one of them said. "I thought somebody shot you. Where's Yoko? When you getting back with Paul?"

The rest of them burst into sharp laughter.

Jerks, he thought, heading immediately over toward the center fountain, where a street comedian was giving a performance. Yeah, the fate of the world was a real rip, wasn't it? He wouldn't let those assholes get to him. He just needed to hit on the right person and things would start rolling. Persistence was the name of the game.

People averted their eyes as he approached them. Not one person would take a flyer. What the hell was this? he wondered.

It was fifteen fruitless minutes later when a petite woman walking past took the flyer from his hand.

Finally, the man thought. His smile collapsed as the woman crumpled it and dropped it to the paved path. He ran forward and scooped it up before he caught up to her.

"The least you could do was wait until you were out of sight before you threw it out in a garbage can," he said as he whirled in front of her. "You have to litter, too?"

"I'm . . . sorry?" the woman said, pulling the white iPod buds from her ears. She hadn't heard a word he'd said. Were all young people today retarded or something? Didn't they see where everything was heading? Didn't they care?

"You certainly are," he mumbled as she walked off. "You *are* sorry. A sorry excuse for a human being."

He stopped dead when he got back to the park's entrance. Someone had kicked over the stack, and most of the flyers were wafting away under the arch, over the sidewalk, whipping north up Fifth Avenue.

He ran out of the park and chased them for a while. He finally stopped. He felt completely drained and idiotic as he sat on the curb between a couple of parked cars.

He held his head in his hands as he wept. For twenty minutes he cried, listening to the wind, watching the relentless roll of traffic in the street.

Flyers? he thought, sniffling. He thought he could change things with a sheet of paper and a concerned expression? He looked down at the antique jeans jacket he'd taken from the back of his closet. So proud that it still fit. He really was a complete fool.

There was only one thing that could get people to sit up straight, only one thing that would open their eyes.

Only one thing then.

And only one thing now.

He nodded, finally resolving himself. He wasn't going to be getting any help. He had to do it himself. Fine. Enough of this nonsense. The clock was ticking. He didn't have any more time to fool the fuck around.

He discovered he was still holding on to a crumpled flyer. He smoothed it out on the cold pavement beside him, took out a pen, and made a vital correction. It snapped like an unfurled flag as he let the wind take it from his fingers.

The broad man with the graying hair wiped his eyes as the sheet he'd written on caught high on the corner lamppost behind him.

The word LOVE in the title had been X'ed out. Against an ash-gray sky above him it now said,

Blood CAN CHANGE THE WORLD!

Part One

ASHES TO ASHES

Chapter 1

BOUND IN THE dark, Jacob Dunning thought about all the things he would give for a shower.

All his possessions? Done. One of his toes? In a heartbeat. One of his fingers? Hmmm, he thought. Did he really need his left pinkie?

Unidentified mudlike filth stuck to his cheek, his hair. Wearing only his NYU T-shirt and boxers, the handsome brown-haired college freshman lay on a soiled concrete floor in a very tight space.

An angry industrial hum raged in the vague distance. He was blindfolded, and his hands were cuffed to a pipe behind him. A gag around his mouth was knotted tight against the hollow indentation at the base of his skull.

The indentation was called the *foramen magnum*, he knew. It was where your spinal cord passed into your skull. Jacob had learned about it in anatomy class a month or so ago. NYU was step one in his lifelong dream to become a doctor. His father had an 1862 edition of *Gray's Anatomy* in his study, and ever since he was a little kid, Jacob had loved going through it. Kneeling in his father's great padded office chair with his chin in his hands, he'd spend hours poring over the elegant, fascinating sketches, the topography of the human body shaded and named like distant lands, like treasure maps.

Jacob sobbed at the safe, happy memory. A drop of lukewarm water landed on the back of his neck and dripped down his spine. The itch of it was unbearable. He would get sores soon if he wasn't able to stand. Bedsores, staph infection, disease.

The last thing he remembered was leaving Conrad's, an Alphabet City bar that didn't care about fake IDs. After a monstrously long chem lab, he'd been trying to chat up Heli, a stunning Finnish girl from his class. But after his fifth mojito, his tongue was losing speed. He'd called it a night when he noticed she was talking more to the male model of a bartender than to him.

His memory seemed to stop at the point when he

stepped outside. How he got from there to here he couldn't recall.

For the billionth time, he tried to come up with a scenario in which everything turned out all right. His favorite was that it was a fraternity thing. A bunch of jocks had mistaken him for some other freshman, and this was a really messed-up hazing incident.

He started weeping. Where were his clothes? Why would somebody take his jeans, his socks and shoes? The scenarios in his head were too black to allow light to enter. He couldn't fool himself. He was in the deepest shit of his young life.

He banged his head on the pipe he was chained to as he heard a sound. It was the distant boom of a door. He felt his heart boom with it. His breath didn't seem to know if it wanted to come in or go out.

He was pretty much convulsing when he made out a jangle interspersed with the steady approach of footsteps. He suddenly thought of the handyman at his parents' building, the merry jingle of keys that bounced off his thigh. Skinny Mr. Durkin, who always had a tool in his hand. Hope gave him courage. It was a friend, he decided. Somebody who would save him.

"Hppp!" Jacob screamed from behind the gag.

The footsteps stopped. A lock clacked open, and cool air passed over the skin of his face. The gag was pulled off.

"Thank you! Oh, thank you! I don't know what happened. I—"

Jacob's breath blasted out of him as he was hit in the stomach with something tremendously hard. It was a steel-toed boot, and it seemed to knock his stomach clear through his spine.

Oh, God, Jacob thought, his head scraping the stone floor as he dry-heaved in filth. *Dear God, please help me.*

Chapter 2

JACOB WAS UNCUFFED and pulled roughly for twenty or so steps and slammed into a hard-backed seat. Light spiked his eyes as his blindfold was sliced away, and his hands were cuffed again behind his back.

He was in a child's school desk in a vast, windowless space. In front of him was an old-fashioned wooden rolling blackboard with nothing written on it. Behind him was a cold presence that lifted the hairs from his neck.

Jacob sobbed silently as a lighter hissed. The faintly spicy scent of tobacco smoke filled the air.

"Good morning, Master Dunning," said a voice behind him.

It was a man's voice. The man sounded perfectly sane, highly educated, in fact. He reminded him of a popular English teacher he'd had at Horace Mann, Mr. Manducci.

Hey, wait. Maybe it *was* Mr. Manducci. He always did seem a little too, er, friendly with some of the male students. Could this be a kidnapping or something? Jacob's CEO father was extremely wealthy.

Jacob could actually feel the relief emit from his pores. He decided he'd take a kidnapping at this point. Ransom, being released. He was down with that. Please be a kidnapping, he found himself thinking.

"My family has money, sir," Jacob said, carefully trying to keep the terror out of his voice and failing.

"Yes, they do," the man said pleasantly. He could have been the DJ for a classical music station. "That's precisely the problem. They have too much money and too little sense. They own a Mercedes McLaren, a Bentley—oh, and a Prius. How green of them. You can thank their hypocrisy for bringing you here. Unfortunately for you, your father seems to have forgotten his Exodus twenty, verse five: 'For I, the Lord your God, am a jealous God, visiting the iniquity of the fathers upon the sons.' "

Jacob twitched violently in the hard chair as a

stainless-steel pistol barrel softly caressed his right cheek.

"Now I'm going to ask you some questions," his captor said. "Your answers are very, very important. You've heard of pass-fail, haven't you?"

The pistol jabbed hard into Jacob's face, its hammer cocking with a sharp click.

"This test you're about to take is pass-die. Now, question one: What was your nanny's name?"

Who? My nanny? Jacob thought. What the hell was this?

"R-R-Rosa?" Jacob said.

"That's right. Rosa. So far, so good, Master Dunning. Now, what was her last name?"

Oh, shit, Jacob thought. Abando? Abrado? Something. He didn't know. The sweet, silly woman that he had played hide-and-seek with. Who'd fed him after school. Rosa, pressing her warm cheek against his as she helped him blow out the candles on his birthday cake. How could he not know her last name?

"Time's up," the man sang.

"Abrado?" Jacob said.

"Not even close," the man said in disgust. "Her name was Rosalita Chavarria. She was a person, you see. She actually had a first *and* a last name. Just like you. She was flesh and blood. Just like you. She died last year, you know. A year after your parents fired her because she was becoming forgetful, she went back to her home country. Which leads us to our third question: What was Rosa's home country?"

How the hell had this guy known about Rosa's termination? Who was this? A friend of hers? He didn't sound Hispanic. Again, *what* was this?

"Nicaragua?" Jacob tried.

"Incorrect again. She was from Honduras. A month after she returned to a one-room shack owned by her sister, she had to go for a hysterectomy. In a substandard hospital outside of Tegucigalpa, she was given a tainted transfusion of blood and contracted HIV. Honduras has the highest concentration of AIDS in the Western Hemisphere. Did you know that? Sure you did.

"Now, question four: What is the average life span in Honduras for an HIV-positive person? I'll give you a hint. It's a hell of a lot less than the fifteen years it is in this country."

Jacob Dunning began to cry.

"I don't know. How would I know? Please."

"That won't do, Jacob," the man said, jamming and twisting the barrel of the gun painfully against his teeth. "Perhaps I'm not making myself clear enough. There'll be no Ivy League A in this class. No tutors. No helpful strategies to maximize your score. You can't cheat, and the results are ultimate. This is a test that you've had your whole life to study for, but I have the feeling you were slacking off. So I'd try to think a little bit harder. HIV-positive life span in Honduras! Answer now!"

Chapter 3

IT WAS THE Catholic grammar school version of March Madness in Holy Name's gym that Sunday around noon. A deafening chaos of ringing basketballs, screaming cheerleaders, and howling sugar-crazed kids rolling over the laminated hardwood on Heelys rose to the angel-carved rafters.

In addition to the noise, it was overly hot, dusty, and crowded, and I couldn't have been happier.

I found myself where I always do when chaos is present, smack-dab in the middle of it. With a whistle around my neck, I was standing at center court, overseeing layup and passing drills as our JV squad, the Holy Name Bulldogs, warmed up. St. Ann's, our crosstown rival from Third Avenue, was doing the same at the opposite end of the court.

Having one son, Ricky, on the varsity squad and another, Eddie, on the JV, I'd somehow found myself nodding in the affirmative when I was asked by the principal, Sister Sheilah, to replace the JV's coach. At first I'd been reluctant. Hello? Single dad, ten kids? Like I didn't have enough to do? But Sister Sheilah can smell a sucker like me from two miles away.

From ball-handling drills to doing the Xs and Os on the chalkboard to even putting away the folding chairs after the game, I'd actually come to get a kick out of coaching. I don't know if any of my 0-and-6 Bulldogs were NBA-bound, but witnessing them gain confidence in themselves and watching the magic that came from going from a bunch of individuals to a somewhat cohesive team, I guess you could do worse things with a Sunday.

The crowd had become so loud at the tip-off that I almost didn't hear the phone going off at my hip. I didn't recognize the number as work, but that didn't mean much. We rotated weekends on my new squad. Guess whose weekend this was?

"Bennett here," I screamed into it.

"Mike, it's Carol. Carol Fleming."

Damn, I thought, closing my eyes. I knew it. Carol was my new boss. Well, my new boss's boss actually. Her name was Chief Carol Fleming. She was the commanding officer of the NYPD's Special Investigative Division, which would have been a big deal even if she weren't the first woman ever to hold the job.

In January, I'd been rotated out of Manhattan North Homicide to the Major Case Squad under her command. Although I preferred Homicide, I had to admit that Major Case, which investigated high-profile bank robberies, art thefts, and kidnappings, wasn't exactly putting me to sleep.

"What's up, boss?" I said.

"We have a possible kidnapping uptown. You need to see April Dunning at One West Seventy-second Street, apartment ten B. Her son, Jacob, seems to be missing. Jacob's father, Donald Dunning, is founder and CEO of—"

"Latvium and Company, the multinational pharmaceutical company," I finished for her. "I've heard of him."

I'd actually read about him in a *Forbes* magazine at my kids' dentist's office. Dunning was a billionaire, and one of the mayor's golfing buddies. I could see where this was heading.

"How old is his kid, Jacob?"

"Eighteen," the chief said.

"Eighteen!?" I said. "Jacob's not missing. He's eighteen."

"I know what it sounds like, Mike. Somebody with City Hall juice looking for their probably party-hearty kid. Be that as it may, I still need you to check it out. Get back to me as soon as you can."

I wrote down the time and address on the back of my player list after I hung up. Find somebody else's kid? I thought. I had trouble enough keeping track of my own. I waved over Seamus, who was booing furiously as one of the St. Ann's players hit a three-pointer.

"Putting me in, Coach, are ya?" my wiseass grandfather priest said in his Guinness-thick brogue. "I keep telling ya I still got game."

I shook my head.

"Listen, Monsignor. I need to check on something, hopefully very quickly. Fill in for me until I get back. On second thought, just stand here and don't say or do anything. Please."

"Finally," Seamus said, gleefully snatching the clipboard from me and rolling up the sleeves of his black shirt. "Maybe we'll win one this time."

Chapter 4

ONE WEST 72nd Street turned out to be the Dakota, the famous Gothic castle-like building where John Lennon had lived before he was shot in front of it. It was also the place where the lady who gives birth to the devil in *Rosemary's Baby* lived, I remembered cheerfully. The good omens just kept on coming this afternoon.

I passed the building and left my van up around the next corner on Columbus and walked back along 72nd. If in the unlikely case this was a kidnapping, it already could be under surveillance. I definitely did not want to advertise that the family had contacted the police.

I passed through a wrought-iron gate at the

Dakota's entrance. Its double-wide arched entryway was the very spot where Chapman had killed the ex-Beatle, shooting him in the back before he could get into the lobby entrance up a short set of stairs to the right. The building was a popular sightseeing tour stop. Yoko, who still lived here, had to be overjoyed when she saw people looking around for bullet holes.

The heavy brass barred door opened as I reached the top. A portly Asian doorman in a hunter green suit coat and hat stood beside an ALL VISITORS MUST BE ANNOUNCED sign.

"I'm here to see the Dunnings," I said, discreetly showing him my shield.

After I was announced, an elderly hall man appeared and guided me through the lobby. The walls had the richest, darkest mahogany paneling I'd ever seen. A massive ballroom chandelier and brass wall sconces softly lit the intricately detailed ceiling moldings and white travertine marble floor.

The hall man, in turn, passed me off to an elevator man. Upstairs, a diminutive butler waved me in through the open door of 10 B.

Through the nearly double-height French doors, I could see the whole way through the Dunnings' apartment to Central Park. The grand rooms were arrayed in the classic enfilade design, allowing more than one way into each room so guests could avoid the servants. The wood floors, like the paneled walls, were Cuban mahogany. They were laid out in a herringbone pattern with what looked like a black-walnut trim.

A striking black-haired woman came quickly down the long corridor of the apartment. She was wearing a rumpled blue evening dress, and even from a distance, the agony in her fine-boned face was unmistakable. My annoyance at being called in dissipated as my heart went out to her. Even with her elegant clothes and her surroundings, she was just a concerned mom sick with worry.

"Thank God you've come. Detective Bennett, is it?" she said with an English accent. "It's my son, Jacob. Something's happened to him."

"I'm here to help you find him, ma'am," I said as reassuringly as I could while I took out my notebook. "When was the last time you saw or spoke to Jacob?"

"I spoke to him three days ago. Jacob lives at school. At NYU. Hayden Hall, right alongside Washington Square Park. My husband is still down there with my father. They've spoken to his friends, and no one has seen him since Friday. Not his roommate. No one."

Maybe he met a cute girl, I felt like saying to her.

"Not seeing someone for a few days might not necessarily mean something's wrong, Mrs. Dunning. Is there a specific reason why you think something's happened to him?"

"My husband and I had our twenty-fifth wedding anniversary last night at Le Cirque. We'd planned it with Jacob for months. Jacob's grandfather flew in from Bordeaux for the occasion. Jacob would not have missed it. He is our only child. You don't understand how close we are. He would not have missed our special event or the rare chance to see his grandfather."

I was starting to understand her concern. What she was telling me did seem strange.

"Did he say anything to you when you last spoke to him? Anything odd? Someone new he might have met or—"

That's when the phone on the antique sideboard beside her rang. She stared in horror at the caller ID number, then at me as it rang again.

"I don't know that number," she said, raw panic in her voice. "I don't know that number!"

"That's okay," I said, trying to calm her down. I scratched down the number, and let my instincts kick in.

"Listen, April. Look at me. If it's someone involved

with Jacob being gone—I don't think it is, but if it is—you need to ask them exactly what you need to do in order to get your son back, okay? And if you can, say that you want to speak to Jacob."

Tears were streaming down her face as the phone rang again. She used a shaking fist to wipe them away before she grabbed the receiver. I listened at an extension in the adjacent study. I pressed the phone's answering machine's Record button as I lifted the receiver.

"Yes? This is April Dunning."

"I have Jacob," a strangely serene voice said. "Listen."

There was a click and hum on the line and then what sounded like a recording.

"Question number nine: If you were born in Sudan, what would be your chances of living to forty? And what does that have to do with your cute little red iPod nano?"

"I don't know," a young man sobbed. "Stop. Please stop."

The recording clicked off.

"You'll receive instructions in exactly three hours," the calm voice said. "Follow them to the letter or you'll never see your son alive again. No police. No FBI."

The connection was cut. I was hanging up the

extension when there was a crash in the hallway. Mrs. Dunning was kneeling on the herringbone floor, sobbing inconsolably.

"It's Jacob," she moaned. "That bastard has my Jacob."

The butler arrived a step before me and helped her into a chair.

I speed-dialed the chief. Unbelievable. This really was a kidnapping. We had no time to waste to get set up. We needed to hustle if we were going to have all our teams in place in three hours. It was going to be close.

I frowned out the window. Down across Central Park West, a tour bus was disembarking, people checking their cameras as they crowded toward the Strawberry Fields John Lennon memorial. My boss's phone rang with a painful slowness as Mrs. Dunning's cries carried through the high-ceilinged rooms.

"C'mon," I said in frustration. "Pick up."

Chapter 5

A BUSINESS JET inbound for Teterboro Airport made FBI special agent Emily Parker duck her copper-colored head as she hurried across the Enterprise parking lot on Route 46 in New Jersey. She stopped for a moment and watched it streak down the runway toward the sleek Gulfstream G300 that had just dropped her off.

She checked her watch after she turned over the engine of her rented Buick LeSabre. It was not yet three. Her boss had called her at twelve-thirty at her home outside Manassas, Virginia. She'd traveled two hundred fifty miles in under two hours.

Now, that's what I call a rush job, she thought. Granted, she was used to the pace, having been in charge of the FBI's northeast regional CARD, or Child Abduction Rapid Deployment, team for two years.

"The ADIC asked me to put my biggest badass on this one, Emily," John Murphy, the special agent in charge of the National Center for the Analysis of Violent Crime, had said to her. "Guess what. You're it."

She hadn't been told much. Only that she was to be a special kidnapping adviser to the NYPD on the abduction of some kid named Jacob Dunning. Jacob's father, Donald Dunning, was actually the one who had sent his Gulfstream for her, which was about as far from normal procedure as you could get.

She was beginning to wonder what kind of special assignment she'd just gotten herself into.

She speed-dialed home as she gunned out of the parking lot. Her brother, Tom, answered his cell on the second ring.

"Just got off the plane," she said. "How's she taking it?"

"Everything's fine. We set up a lemonade stand at the end of the driveway. That's so cute that you guys do that every Sunday."

"That little fibber," Emily cried. "A lemonade stand? Near the street!? Oh, that's just like her. She's got her hooks into you already. I told her no last week. What about the traffic? Are you there? Right now? Who's watching her?"

"Of course I'm here, Em. What do you think, I'm talking to you from a bar?" her brother said. "Me and the Olive are glued together at the hip."

Tom had gotten a job with a defense contractor in Bethesda after getting out of the Marines the month before. He was due to start next week. Renting him the basement apartment in her split-level had turned out to be a win-win stroke of genius, a built-in babysitter. Emily grinned, picturing her precious goofball of a four-year-old, Olivia, out by the end of the cul-de-sac in her winter coat, wondering where the customers were.

"Do we even have lemonade?" she said.

"I made a command decision and substituted Kool-Aid."

"Kool-Aid!? That's pure processed sugar and dye. Kool-Aid! She can only have one glass. One."

"You sound like I'm force-feeding her antifreeze. Besides, she's not drinking it, she's trying to sell it. Try not to have an aneurysm, please. I survived Kabul, I think I can look after the Olive. You have any idea how long you're going to be gone for?"

"Not yet, but I'll let you know. Kiss her for me,

okay, Tom? I know you can take perfect care of her. I just get nuts leaving ever since . . . you know."

"The D-I-V-O—"

"Shut up, Tom, would you? She can spell better than you. Good-bye."

After her divorce the year before, Emily had taken a transfer to ride a desk at CASMIRC, the Bureau's Child Abduction and Serial Murder Investigative Resource Center, because it had regular hours. The case files that came in for review from every corner of the country weren't exactly light reading, but when you were a profiler, you had to take the work where you could find it.

The job was ideal for taking care of Olivia, but to say Emily was starting to climb the beige walls of her cubicle in the basement office at the FBI Academy would be putting it mildly.

Emily smiled as she dropped the Buick's hammer up the entrance for the turnpike, cutting off a tricked-out Cadillac SUV. Off to her right, New York City's metal-and-glass skyline appeared like a vision over the Jersey swamp.

Still got it, she thought, keeping the gas on the floor. Gangway, badass coming through!

Chapter 6

I DON'T THINK I'd ever been as proud of the NYPD. In only two hours, we'd managed to get everything up and running.

I, two other Major Case detectives, and a PD tech were stationed at the Dunnings' apartment. Another team of detectives was busy scouring NYU to find out where Jacob had last been seen. A third surveillance team, made up of undercover Emergency Service Unit tactical guys, was spread around outside the Dakota, especially the Strawberry Fields area in Central Park.

After Lennon was shot, the building had become a kind of morbid landmark, like the grassy knoll in Dallas. Maybe it was just a coincidence that Jacob lived here, but for the time being, we couldn't rule out the pull of the place for some unbalanced person.

An NYPD TARU tech had already spliced recording equipment onto the Dunnings' line. The phone company had been contacted and was ready with something called a time-stop trace. Its billing computer would zip through its millions of circuits that were operational at the exact second the Dunnings' phone rang and find the one calling the apartment.

All we had to do now was the hard part. To sit and wait until four o'clock. Sit and wait and pray.

My heart rattled like an alarm clock in my chest cavity when the phone rang at three-thirty. It took me a long second to realize that it wasn't the apartment phone but the building's intercom buzzer in the kitchen.

Armando, the butler, rushed to answer it.

"There's an FBI agent in the lobby, sir," he called to Donald Dunning.

What?! I thought. *Who called the FBI?*

"Send her up," Dunning said. Turning to me, he added, "Did I forget to tell you? I called the Justice Department when I was down at Jacob's dorm. The attorney general, Fred Carroll, dated my sister in college. He's sending in his best, he told me. You can work together with the FBI, right?"

"Sure," I said, exchanging uncertain glances with Detectives Ramirez and Schultz, the other members of my team. We had everything ready to go. Now the Feds were here? What did that mean?

We exchanged much happier looks as a tall, auburn-haired woman came through the door two minutes later. Good-looking women, even ones who were turf-invading FBI agents, were always a pleasant surprise.

She spoke to Donald Dunning and his wife briefly in the foyer before stepping into the study.

"Emily Parker," she said, offering her hand. She had a slight southern or maybe midwestern accent. "Mike Bennett, is it? I can see by your surprise that no one told you I was coming. Of course not. My boss is calling your boss or something.

"I know you guys are as good as we are. I'm not here in any way to take the case away from you. Just here to coordinate resources you guys might not have, get you on the front of the line for databases and such. This is odd, I know, to come all the way up from Washington and—"

"Wait, what?" I said. "From Washington? Why didn't they just send someone from Twenty-six Fed?"

"Because I wanted the best," Donald Dunning

said, coming in behind her. "You solved two. That's what Freddy told me. You got two kidnapped kids back safely."

"It was actually three, but yes."

Okay, now I saw where this was going. Dunning was flexing his considerable muscle, using his juice to pull out all the stops.

He obviously didn't realize the strange kind of animal that an investigation in New York City is. I'm sure Homecoming Queen Emily Parker kicked ass out in those big square states where they didn't have things like subways and Brooklyn and eight million people. The NYPD, despite its gruff demeanor, Bugs Bunny accent, and lack of executive hair, was the investigative equal of any law enforcement agency, especially when in its own backyard.

But I knew if I made some kind of jurisdictional stink, the Feds could invoke the Federal Kidnapping Statute and actually take over the case.

Instead of ranting and raving, I stood there politely holding my tongue and keeping a stiff smile.

Chapter 7

"MR. DUNNING, I'D like to speak to you and your wife further in a moment," Agent Parker said. Her demeanor was the perfect mix of directness and caring. "I just need to go over a few things with Detective Bennett first. Will you be in the kitchen?"

"Oh, of course," Dunning mumbled before leaving the study.

That was about as polite a "get lost" as I'd ever seen. I was impressed. Maybe Agent Parker had some chops after all.

She closed the French doors tightly behind him.

"Did you check out the Dunnings for any domestic violence complaints or criminal records?" she said.

I saw where she was going. It had to be verified

from the start that it was, in fact, a stranger kidnapping and not a cover-up for a murder or something else. Step one was ruling out the family. I was way ahead of her.

"Both clean," I said, nodding. "We're still checking out the staff. How did the Dunnings' demeanor seem to you? About right?"

"The mom seems to be in a dissociative fugue, and the father looks like he's just chugged a quart of battery acid," Parker said with a shrug. "In this case, both typical responses. You want me to toss their name at the White Collar Squad just in case? Can't hurt to check out any recent debt or insurance activity. We could even look up psychiatric history, if any."

Wow, I thought. Talk about trusting no one and nothing. I liked that in a cop.

"Do it," I said.

She took a pad from her briefcase and scribbled on it.

"Any witnesses to the abduction?" Parker said.

"None," I said. "A girl in one of his classes has Jacob leaving some shithole in Alphabet City at one o'clock in the morning Saturday."

"Alphabet City?" Parker said.

"A neighborhood near his school," Detective Schultz piped in.

"A skanky one," added Ramirez.

"Go on," she said with a nod.

"We're thinking he was grabbed right then because by the look of things, Jacob never made it back to his dorm room," I said. "We already interviewed his roommate and tossed the building. Nothing. If he went on a trip, he forgot to tell everyone he knows."

I handed her the rough copy of the victimology report I'd already done, along with a current photograph.

"This report is excellent," Parker said, turning the pages with an impressed nod. "Physical characteristics, behavior personality, and family dynamics. This NYPD thing doesn't work out, we could use you down in Quantico. Tell me about the contact with the kidnapper."

I went to the desk and pressed Play on the answering machine. Special Agent Parker squinted with surprise as the strange question-and-answer recording echoed through the room.

I clicked it off when it was over.

"Parents confirmed the person being questioned is Jacob," I said. "Have you ever heard anything like that before?"

Parker shook her head.

"Not even close," she said. "Sounded like an odd game show or something. Have you?"

I let out a frustrated breath.

"Sort of," I said. "About a year ago, there was this guy who called himself the Teacher. Like this guy, he would blather on about our unjust society. Right before he blew holes in people."

"Of course. The spree killer. The plane that crashed in New York Harbor, right? I read about that," Parker said.

I nodded.

"Wait! The cop in the plane! Bennett, my God, that was you?"

I nodded again as she took that in.

"So, you think this is some sort of copycat?" Parker said.

I took a breath, remembering how hard I'd knocked on death's door.

"For this family's sake," I said, shaking the last drop of coffee from my cup, "I hope not."

Chapter 8

EVERY TWO MINUTES or so, Armando came in to refill our china cups from a polished silver coffee urn. I'd told him twice that he didn't need to go to all the trouble, but he'd turned a deaf ear to us. He seemed as concerned about Jacob as his parents were.

The whirring sound of a mixer started in the kitchen. From the study, I saw Jacob's mother, tears pouring down her cheeks, her hair mussed, her evening gown covered in flour, open the fridge and go back to the island, carrying eggs.

Armando made the sign of the cross.

"Poor Mrs. D, always she bake when she is upset," he said in a whisper.

I'd shown Jacob's room to Agent Parker and had just started going over potential media strategies when Detective Schultz called me over to the study's window. Outside the Dakota's main entrance, a black Chevy Suburban with tinted windows had its blue police light flashing on its dashboard.

I immediately called down to the ESU guys doing surveillance on the street.

"What the hell is going on down there?" I said. "Kill those lights. Who is that jackass? This is supposed to be an undercover operation."

"Someone from the mayor's office," an ESU sergeant stationed in the lobby said. "She's on her way up."

A minute later, a sharp-featured fifty-something woman with a salon-perfected blond bob came through the apartment's front door.

"April! I came straight here when I heard the news," she said.

Mrs. Dunning seemed taken aback as she was engulfed in the tall woman's viselike embrace. So did Mr. Dunning when he was given the same treatment.

"Christ, this is all we need," I mumbled.

It was the first deputy mayor, Georgina Hottinger. Before being promoted to the mayor's second in line, she'd been in charge of the New York Improvement Fund, which roped wealthy individuals into paying for city events. Which would have been useful had this been a charity function instead of a kidnapping investigation.

"Who's in charge here?" she commanded as she burst into the study. I guess she was through with the air- and ass-kissing.

"I am. Mike Bennett. Major Case Squad," I said.

"Every development in this case is to be sent immediately to my office. And I mean every one. The Dunnings will be shown every imaginable courtesy in their time of need, first and foremost being their privacy."

Staring into her ice-pick blue eyes, I suddenly remembered the nickname the City Hall press corps had given Hottinger. Still resembling the ballerina in the San Francisco ballet that she'd once been, the take-no-prisoners politico was called the "Barbed-Wire Swan."

"This woman is a personal friend of mine, Detective," Hottinger continued. "So I hope we're clear on how this thing is to be run. I'll be holding you personally responsible for any fuckups. Why are we running this, by the way? Are we even capable? I thought kidnappings were a federal offense. Has the FBI been informed?"

"Yes, they have, actually," Emily Parker said, glaring at her. "I'm Special Agent Parker. And you are?"

Georgina whirled around, looking like she wanted to give Emily a roundhouse pirouette to the jaw.

"Me?" Hottinger said. "Oh, no one, really. I just happen to be the one who's in charge of the capital of the world until the mayor comes back on Tuesday. You have any other stupid questions, Agent?"

"Just one," Emily said, nonplussed. "Did it occur to you when you pulled up with your lights flashing that the person responsible for abducting Jacob could now be watching this building? They demanded that no police be contacted. Now it looks like you've blown that. I believe you were saying something about fuckups?"

I got between the two ladies before the fur started flying. And they say men can't get along. I decided I was starting to like Parker a little.

"I'll be in contact with your office, Deputy Mayor. As soon as I hear anything, so will you," I said, guiding her out into the hall. "We're still waiting for the perpetrator to call back, so if you'll let us get back to work."

Parker was blowing out a flushed breath as the apartment's front door slammed behind Hottinger.

"This political personal-service crap pisses me off

to no end, Mike," Parker said. "First the attorney general, now the mayor's office is involved? I actually got here on Dunning's jet, did I tell you that? Do you think for a minute that there'd be this much effort if some poor nobody kid was abducted?"

"Probably not," I said. "But think about it. If your kid were in danger, wouldn't you pull every string you had?"

In the kitchen, Mrs. Dunning slammed a muffin tin hard enough to shake the glass in the French doors.

"You're right. I would," Parker said with a nod. "Can we at least both agree that the deputy mayor is one rabid bitch?"

"Now, on that one," I said with a laugh, "I'm with you one hundred percent."

Chapter 9

AT 3:55, DONALD Dunning sat down at the Chippendale desk in the study. On it were chess sets chiseled in marble, leather-bound books, antique tin soldiers, a seashell inlaid with gold. But his eyes, along with everyone else's, were locked squarely on the phone.

It rang at the stroke of four. It was a different number from the first call, a 718 area code this time.

Dunning wiped his sweating hands on his slacks before he lifted the receiver.

"This is Donald Dunning. Please tell me what I have to do to get my son back. I'll do whatever you want," he said.

"You mean except for calling the police when I

told you not to?" the calm voice from the first call said. "Put them on the line. I know they're there. Try to fool me again, and I'll FedEx you a piece of Jacob in a biohazard bag."

Dunning's face went a shade of white I'd never seen before. His lips moved silently. I nodded to him that it was okay as I took the phone from his shaking hand.

"This is Mike Bennett. I'm a detective with the NYPD," I said. "How's Jacob? Is he okay?"

"We'll discuss Jacob in due time, Mike," the kidnapper said. "Did you hear that officious blowhard? His son's life lies naked in my bare hands, and he thinks he can still give orders?"

"I think Mr. Dunning is just upset because he misses his son," I said as I took out my notepad. "You're obviously holding all the cards. All we want to know is how we can get Jacob back."

"Funny you say that," the kidnapper said. "About holding all the cards. I wish I really were, instead of absolute assholes like Dunning. Then this kind of thing wouldn't be necessary."

Former employee? I wrote on the pad. *Disgruntled? Personal vendetta?*

There was a pause, and then a strange sound started. At first I thought that I heard laughing, but after a second I realized the kidnapper was sobbing uncontrollably.

I don't know what I had been expecting, but it definitely wasn't tears.

Unstable, I scribbled on the pad.

"What is it?" I said after a little while. "What's making you so upset?"

"This world," the kidnapper said in a choked-up whisper. "How messed up it is. The greed and rampant injustice. There is so much we could do, but we just sit by and let it all go down the drain. Dunning could save twenty lives with what he pays for his shoes. Latvium stock rises on the corpses of the world's poor."

"Don't they also create drugs that save lives?" I said. Rule number one in negotiating is to keep the person talking. "I thought a lot of big drug companies actually give drugs away to Third World countries."

"That's just bullshit for the multimillion-dollar marketing campaign," the kidnapper said wearily. "The donated drugs are crap. Often expired. Sometimes deadly. In reality, the most common way Latvium interacts with Third World citizens is when it uses them as guinea pigs. The cherry on top is the way it launders its profits through offshore banks, using copyright laws and shell companies to avoid paying American taxes. Look it up, Mike. It's common knowledge. Congress looks the other way. I wonder why. Can you say *lobbyists*? Can you say *institutional corruption*?"

The kidnapper sighed.

"Are you that dense? Latvium is a multinational company. The sole purpose of multinational corporations in every industry is the production of fabulous wealth for its upper management. National responsibility and human lives are asides to men like him. Always have been. Always will be."

He did have something of a point, I thought. He was actually kind of persuasive. His voice sounded cultured, like an academic's. *Intelligent,* I wrote on my pad.

"But the wind is blowing in a different direction now," he continued. "The hand of destiny knocks upon the door. That's why I'm doing this. To wake people up. To make them rethink the way in which they conduct themselves. Because these wings are no longer wings to fly but merely vans to beat the air. The air which is now thoroughly small and dry. Smaller and dryer than the will. Teach us to care and not to care. Teach us to sit still."

God, now he was talking gibberish. I underlined *Unstable*. Beside it, I wrote, *Drugs? Schizoid? Psychotic? Hearing voices?*

"Now getting back to Jacob," I said. "Could we speak to him?"

He let out a deep breath. Then he gave me by far the largest shock of our conversation.

"I'll do better than that. You can have him back, Mike," he said.

I stood holding the receiver, stunned.

"You'll have to come for him, though," the voice continued. "Give me your cell phone number. Get in a car. I'll call you in ten minutes."

He hung up after I gave him my number.

"It's over?" Dunning said happily, with surprise. "He's going to give him back? I guess he changed his mind, is that it? He must have realized how crazy this was. April! Honey! Jacob's coming home!"

I watched Dunning run out of the room. He was grasping at any hope now.

Unfortunately, I wasn't as optimistic. The individual who'd taken Jacob seemed highly organized. He wouldn't have gone to all this trouble to just give him back.

What was filling me with even more dread was the way he kept changing the subject when I asked about Jacob.

I could tell by the skeptical look on Parker's face that she was thinking exactly the same thing.

Chapter 10

AN UNMARKED BLACK Impala was gassed and waiting in the cold rain around the corner on Central Park West. In the front seat, I handed Parker one of the Kevlar vests draped across the dashboard and slipped into the other.

We would be the lead car, with Schultz and Ramirez loosely tailing us. Aviation had been called, and a Bell 206 was en route from Floyd Bennett Field in Brooklyn for high-altitude covert surveillance.

"What was that about the wings?" I said to Parker as we sat there waiting for the kidnapper to call back.

"I think it was a poem. It's on the tip of my tongue. My college English professor would kill me."

"Where'd you go to school?" I said.

"UVA."

"Virginia. So that explains the down-home accent."

"Accent?" Emily drawled. "Y'all Yankees are the ones with the accent."

An FBI agent with a sense of humor, I thought, listening to the drumroll of rain on the roof. What were the odds?

I put my phone on speaker and was adjusting the no-hands microphone when it rang. It was yet a different number, I noticed, a Long Island 516 area code, the third number so far. Maybe our kidnapper owned a cell phone store, I thought as I folded it open.

"Listen to my instructions. Go exactly where I say," the kidnapper told me. "Take the Central Park traverse to the East Side."

I took a breath as we pulled out. It started to rain harder. Against the gray sky, the bare trees atop the park's stone walls looked black in the rain.

A few minutes later, I said, "I'm coming up on Fifth Avenue now."

"Keep going to Park Avenue and make an uptown left."

I sped out of the park down two tony East Side blocks and screeched through the red light.

"I'm on Park Avenue," I said.

"Welcome to the silk-stocking district, Mike," the kidnapper said. "Holy one-zero-zero-two-one. Did you know you're now driving through the highest concentration of wealth in the richest country on earth? In the salons above you, more money is paid over to both of our sham political parties than in any other place."

We drove on. The only sound in the car was the windshield wipers. I didn't see any salons. All the buildings outside were just gray smudges.

The last high-profile kidnapping Major Case had handled involved a garment factory owner who was kidnapped back in '93. They'd pulled him, filthy and starving but, thankfully, still alive, out of a hole in the ground along the West Side Highway. I wondered what kind of hole Jacob was in now. Most of all, I hoped the eighteen-year-old was still alive when we pulled him out of it.

"Where are you?" the kidnapper said.

"I'm at One Hundred and Tenth and Park."

"Spanish Harlem," he said. "See how quickly it all turns to shit? When Park Avenue ends, head over the Madison Avenue Bridge into the Bronx."

The tires slipped for a gut-wrenching second as we sped over the wet, rusting bridge. The Harlem River beneath was brownish green and looked almost solid, as if you could walk across it.

"I'm in the Bronx now," I announced when I reached the other side of the river.

"Take the Grand Concourse north."

We slid past project after project. We were passing alongside a lot the size of a city block, filled with stacks of old tires, when the kidnapper started in with more commentary.

"Did you know that the Grand Concourse was supposed to be the Park Avenue of the Bronx?" he said. "Look at it now. At the burned-out, marble-trimmed windows. At the granite facades painted over with graffiti memorials for slain drug dealers. How did we let this happen, Mike? Have you ever asked yourself that? How did we let the world become what it is?"

Soon the area became wall-to-wall decayed tenements. We were in the Forty-sixth Precinct now, I knew. "The Alamo," they called it. It was the smallest, but the most drug-infested, precinct in the city.

As I stared out at the inner-city blight, flashes of Jacob's room came to mind. The cross-country-running trophies he kept in the back of his closet, the Dave Matthews Band ticket stubs on his dresser, the shiny Les Paul guitar that hung on his wall. Despite his age, he was a kid, really. I gritted my teeth. This was no place for any kid.

"I'm coming up to One Hundred and Ninety-sixth," I said.

"Good work," the kidnapper said. "You're almost there, Mike. Go right onto One Hundred Ninety-sixth. You're really close now. Make a left onto Briggs Avenue."

I cupped the phone mic.

"What are you packing?" I said over to Parker.

"Glock forty-caliber," she said.

"Unsnap your holster," I said.

Chapter 11

A HARD-LOOKING BLACK kid in a new North Face jacket twirled a Gucci umbrella on the corner. Behind him down the block at regular intervals, more menacing figures in dark hoodies stood on the thresholds of the run-down brick buildings. Apparently even the rain couldn't put a damper on Briggs Avenue's open-air drug market.

"*Whoop, whoop,*" came the warning cry as I turned the car onto the avenue, and my unmarked was immediately made. "Five-oh," one teen spotter hollered down the block helpfully to his coworkers through cupped hands. "Yo, Five-oh!"

I scanned the gloomy block uncertainly. The

narrow cutout of the avenue extended for at least another two blocks without a cross street.

Where the hell were Schultz and Ramirez? I thought, glancing into my rearview. I felt like a sheriff who'd made a wrong turn into the wrong mountain pass.

"Stop at two-five-oh Briggs," the kidnapper said.

Emily tapped me on the shoulder and pointed at a building up the block. I didn't have time to look for a parking spot. I spun the wheel and bumped the Impala up onto the sidewalk in front of it.

With swirling architectural embellishments around its entrance, 250 Briggs Avenue, like a lot of old Bronx buildings, had once been a stately residence. Since then, one of the entrance's Doric columns had been shattered, and there were smoke stains on the brick above most of the boarded-up windows of the third story.

I got soaked to the bone while I retrieved flashlights from the trunk of the detective car. So did Emily as we walked across the cracked sidewalk and pulled open the building's broken front door.

"I'm here. I'm in the lobby of two-fifty now," I said into the phone. My words echoed eerily back at me as I played the beam over the dim lobby. The walls were marble, but the low ceiling was bloated, pregnant with water stains and mold. A feeling as desolate as my surroundings enveloped me. I had the sudden desperate feeling that time was running out.

Where are you, Jacob? I thought.

"Did you know that people actually live here?" the kidnapper said in my ear. "Rats run through the halls. Some of the tenants on the third floor don't even have doors after a recent fire. Is it any wonder at all that this area has the highest incidence of childhood asthma in the country?

"The slumlord who bought it last year, along with eighty percent of this block, has let it get like this because he's trying to force out the rent-controlled tenants. He bought it at a HUD auction, despite his company's history of thirteen hundred housing-code violations. This is happening here in the richest country on earth, Mike. This is happening right here, right now in America."

"Where is Jacob?" I yelled, ignoring his grating litany. "I'm here. I've done exactly what you said. Where do I go?"

"Out back through the courtyard, go through the laundry room door on your left."

We found a door at the end of the lobby and went back out into the rain. A cracked toilet lid floated beside half a dozen faded phone books in the courtyard's standing water. I scanned the surrounding windows for movement. I wasn't convinced yet that this wasn't a trap.

I handed Emily my flashlight as I drew my gun and pulled open the door in the left-hand wall. I found the lights. No Jacob. Just a rusted-through sink beside an ancient coin-op washing machine.

"Where is he?" I yelled again.

"The stairs on your left. Take them down."

Beyond the washing machine, iron steps descended through a raw concrete stairwell. The beams from our flashlights flickered wildly as we flew down the steps two at a time.

Dank heat hit me like a wall through the door at the bottom. In the distance, a boiler screamed as if it were being tortured. The basement walls looked like hewn stone, and I felt like we were entering a cave. Or a dungeon, I thought.

"This is where I'll have to end our little conversation for now, Mike. Down the hall to your right. Take Jacob away. He's all yours," the kidnapper said and hung up.

Chapter 12

I COVERED EMILY as she jogged ahead. Even in the dimness, I could see her eyes widen in shock as she stuck her light and gun through the right-hand doorway.

I arrived a split second behind her. Emily's flashlight showed a figure slumped over a child's desk. Something stung my cheek as I raced toward it. It was a pull chain. I wrapped my hand around it and yanked.

The hanging bulb clicked on and then swung back and forth, heaving shadows of Jacob's motionless body up and down the raw cement walls.

No! Damn it! Not like this! I thought.

Jacob was in his underwear, and his hands were

cuffed behind his back. I checked for a pulse. Nothing. I scanned frantically for a wound.

"His hair," Emily said quickly behind me. There was a crusted pool of blood at the top of his head. His hair was matted with it.

A bullet wound gaped at the crown of his skull. I turned away. Wiping the sweat from my face, I glanced at the blackboard, the desk, the naked cement wall, and then back at the body.

I ripped my phone from my belt, ready to smash it against the wall. The sick son of a bitch had been leading us along, whispering not-so-sweet nothings in my ear, and the whole time the kid had been dead.

"He lied to us from the get-go," I said, desperately trying to throttle the life out of my RAZR phone. "This kid was long dead when he called. God, I want to nail this son of a bitch."

"I'll hold the nails while you swing the hammer," Emily said, putting a hand on my shoulder. "This is a shock. Maybe we should take a quick breather. Do you want to go up top for some air?"

You better believe I wanted to take a breather. I wanted to get the hell out of that steaming South Bronx crypt.

My thumb found my boss's listing instead.

"Tell me some good news, Mike," Chief Fleming said.

"I wish I could. I'm in the basement of two-five-oh Briggs Avenue. We need the Crime Scene Unit and the medical examiner."

"Goddammit," my boss said. "How?"

"He blew the kid's brains out," I said. "I'd give the notification duty to Georgina Hottinger, if I were you. She likes to play cop with her flashing lights. I wouldn't want to deprive her of getting all the way in on the act."

I met Ramirez and Schultz in the hallway when they finally arrived five minutes later.

"Canvass everyone you can find in this dump," I said. "Especially the super. Roust him and the landlord as well. This guy took his time with this kid down here. I want to know why nobody noticed."

Chapter 13

WHEN I RETURNED, Emily had her jacket off and was hovering over the body. She had her blouse sleeves rolled up and was wearing green rubber surgical gloves she'd gotten from somewhere. Her bag probably. I was impressed.

"The back spatter on the floor here and the lividity in the legs indicate he was killed in the chair," she said without looking up.

I probed Jacob's arm gently with my thumb.

"Looks like a semi-advanced state of rigor," I said. "I'd say he was killed sometime early this morning. The handcuff cuts on the wrists and his scraped knees look like he was treated pretty roughly before he was killed. Tying this in with the question-and-answer stuff from the first call, I'd say this looks like a teacher-student domination fantasy or something."

"Yeah," Emily said, waving away a fly. "Welcome to Hell one-oh-one."

I peered at Jacob's face. He had his mother's dark hair and creamy complexion, his father's blue eyes. Those eyes were frozen open forever now, along with his mouth in a rictus of shock and horror. There was a smudge on his forehead that I hadn't noticed before, a gray mark like a small *X*.

"Hey, Mike," Emily said a second later. She was standing at the other side of the room. "I think you need to see this."

I joined her on the other side of the blackboard. On the back, someone had written:

MEMENTO HOMO, QUIA PULVIS ES,
ET IN PULVEREM REVERTERIS.

"What is that? Latin?" Emily said.

"It is," I said, staring at it. "My Catholic high school's preferred method of torture. *Memento* means 'remember,' I think. *Pulvis* is 'dust.' "

Cold numbed my back like a spinal tap as I suddenly realized its meaning.

" 'Remember that you are dust and to dust you

shall return,' " I cried. "It's what Catholic priests say on Ash Wednesday when you get your ashes. Which must be what's on the kid's forehead. He gave Jacob ashes?"

Emily snapped her rubber-gloved finger loudly.

"Wait a second! That's it. 'Teach us to care and not to care. Teach us to sit still.' The poem is called *Ash Wednesday,* by T. S. Eliot. What does it mean? How does it tie into the kidnapping?"

"I don't know," I said. "But I think the clock just started."

I wiped the sweat out of my eyes.

"Ash Wednesday is only three days away," I said.

Chapter 14

THE SUPER WAS nowhere to be found. The closest occupants to the basement were in a crack house on the second floor, but to no one's surprise, the strung-out inhabitants hadn't noticed anything.

I was happy for the cold rain now as I climbed out of that hot pit. I needed something to wash the smell of death from my clothes, off my skin.

Despite our attempts to keep things under wraps, I spotted the police reporter from the *Post* standing behind the police tape among the half dozen Briggs Avenue drug dealers. Once the word was out, reporters and producers would pounce on Briggs Avenue like sharks on chum. A billionaire's kid getting kidnapped and ritually murdered wasn't just news, it was the next news cycle.

I headed for my car when I spotted the first news van. Media storms were like real ones, I'd found. The only way to truly withstand them was to evacuate immediately.

Emily was coming out of the corner bodega as I got to the car. She took the items from the bag as I cranked the heat in the front seat. Paper towels and a couple of cans of Coke.

"They didn't have any Scotch, but at least it's full sugar," she said, handing me one.

I put the cold can to the back of my neck before I crunched it open.

"*Full* sugar," I said. "I just might have to tell your supervisor about you, Emily Parker. Not for nothing, but you were great in there. You know your way around a body. I thought you were just a kidnapping expert."

"I did time in the Behavioral Analysis Unit as a profiler," she said offhandedly. "Lucky me, huh?"

I watched her rub her hair with a wad of paper towels. It was the color of black cherry soda where it was wet along the nape of her neck, I suddenly noticed.

She paused as the ME's techs brought out Jacob in a plastic bag. They slid him into the back of the beat-up Bronx County Medical Examiner's van parked beside our Impala.

"I lost four," Emily said, staring out the rain-streaked windshield.

"What are you talking about?"

"Dunning was so impressed that I had found three, but nobody told him that I lost four," she said, looking into my eyes. "Actually, five now," she added.

I lifted my soda and took a sip. It wasn't black cherry, which I had a distinct pang for all of a sudden, but the sugar rush would have to do.

"Three for seven," I said. "That's great. If this were baseball, you'd be Ted Williams."

"This isn't baseball, though, is it?" Emily said after a moment.

I took another sip of my Coke and dropped the transmission into reverse to let the death van out.

"You're right," I said as we bumped off the sidewalk onto the wet street. "There's no crying in baseball."

Chapter 15

IT WAS DARK by the time we rolled across the Madison Avenue Bridge and safely back into Manhattan.

Along the way, Emily had called her Bureau boss and dropped the bad news. Then she made another call to what I assumed was her family. It sounded like she was talking to a little kid.

Then and only then did I check her hand for a ring. Yes, men are that dumb. At least I am. There was no ring, which meant what? Maybe she didn't wear one at work. I shouldn't get my hopes up. Was I getting them up? I guessed I was.

As I drove, I called the TARU tech for an update about the phone leads. They'd actually made some headway. The phone numbers recorded at the Dunnings' and the ones to my cell phone were from prepaid cells bought at three different locations in Queens, Manhattan, and Five Towns out on Long Island. Precinct detectives were being sent to interview the salesmen to see if they remembered anything about the purchaser.

My next call back to the Crime Scene guys was less promising. There were no bullet casings or fingerprints anywhere. Our guy had even had the presence of mind to take the piece of chalk he'd used to write the message.

All in all, this animal who'd killed Jacob had been calculated, methodical, and very careful. All negatives from where we sat. I still couldn't get his perfectly inflected PBS voice out of my head.

We were on Fifth Avenue just passing Central Park North when I looked up. I was supposed to drop Emily off at the Hilton near Rockefeller Center, but I decided I couldn't wait any longer. The suspense was killing me about my kids' game. If Seamus had shown me up in the coaching department, I didn't know if I'd be able to live it down.

Emily looked confused as I stopped in front of my building on West End.

"I need to stop at my apartment for a second. I have to, uh, see about something. You want to wait in the car—or what the hell, come up. I'll get you an umbrella and a real Scotch if you need one. I know I do."

Chapter 16

EMILY LOOKED EVEN more confused as my doorman, Kevin, opened the lobby door.

"How much do they pay New York City cops?" she said as we headed for the elevator.

"Very funny," I said. "Don't worry, I'm not on the take. It's a long story, but basically I won real-estate lotto."

You could hear the ruckus as soon as the elevator opened in my foyer.

"Is someone having a party?" Emily said.

I laughed as I opened the door.

"Oh, the party never ends around here," I said.

Everyone was in the living room. Seamus. The teens, the tweens, and the little ones, who were getting bigger and more expensive by the hour. Wall-to-wall people, laughing, fighting, gaming, watching TV. The mosh pit that was my home life.

"Dad!" several of my kids cried when I was eventually noticed.

When I turned back to Emily, I could see that she was beyond confused and now deep in utterly bamboozled territory. I smiled, remaining silent. Teasing her was becoming quite pleasant.

"They're not all yours," she said.

"Except for the priest," I said, making an expansive gesture with my hands. "He's just a loafer."

"Very funny," Seamus said. "We won. So there."

"No!" I yelled, stricken. "No, it's not possible. How? You threatened to excommunicate the other team?"

"No, I tried something you wouldn't know about. Sound coaching techniques. Take that, ya wiseass," Seamus said. "Now how about introducing me to your lovely friend here."

"Emily, meet Father Seamus Bennett, our local pastor, and though I don't like to admit it too often, my grandfather. We're working together on a case, Monsignor. Emily's an FBI agent."

"FBI," Seamus said, impressed, as he shook her hand. "A G-lady in the flesh. Is it true they let you torture suspects now?"

"Just annoying old men," I answered for her.

The kids, finally noticing that there was a stranger in their midst, quieted down and sat staring. Trent, one of our family's many comedians, stepped over like a four-foot-tall butler.

"Hello," he said, offering his hand to Emily. "Welcome to the Bennett home. May I take your coat?"

Emily stared at me as she shook his hand. "Um . . . ," she said.

"How do you do?" said Ricky, getting in on the act. "It's sooo nice of you to come for dinner, ma'am."

"All right, you goofballs. Enough," I said.

Just then, Juliana, my oldest girl, stopped as she came in from the kitchen. She pulled out her ever-present iPod earbuds before turning back for the kitchen.

"Mary Catherine, Dad brought a guest home. Should I set out another plate?"

Mary Catherine appeared a minute later.

"Of course," she said.

"Oh, I couldn't. I wouldn't want to impose, Mrs. Bennett."

"Did you hear what she said?" cried Chrissy. "Hey, everyone. Did you hear that? She called Mary Catherine Mrs. Bennett!"

"I'm sorry?" Emily said, looking at me, raw pleading in her face.

"That's it, you guys. Back off now, and I mean it," I said. I turned to Emily. "It's a long story. Mary Catherine and I aren't married," I started. I laughed suddenly. "That didn't come out right. What I mean to say is—"

"What he means to say is that I work for this crew," Mary Catherine said. "Pleased to meet you," she said, shaking Emily's hand briskly.

"Oh, my mistake," Emily said.

Just then, the saliva-inducing scent of rosemary, garlic, and pepper hit us like a freight train. Emily turned as Juliana placed a massive roasted leg of lamb on the dining room table. It smelled insanely good.

"On Sundays, Mary Catherine pulls out all the stops," I explained.

Emily's eyes went wide as Brian came in carrying mashed potatoes on a platter the size of a toboggan.

"You definitely do not have to stay," I said to Emily. "Don't let these tricksters fool you with their polite routine. We redefine the term *family-style*."

Socky began rubbing himself on Emily's shin.

"But, Daddy, look. Even Socky wants her to stay," said Chrissy, batting her butterfly-wing eyelids up at Emily.

Emily knelt down and finally petted the cat.

"Well, if Socky says I should, I guess I have to," she said.

"In that case, here," I said, pouring Emily a huge glass of red wine. "You're going to need this."

Chapter 17

TRYING TO KEEP her balance amid the swirl of kids and motion in the bright, warm apartment, Emily Parker sipped her wine and smiled.

Incredible, she thought. All these children. So many races. They had to be adopted, right? At least some of them did. And was there a Mrs. Bennett? She'd definitely gotten single vibes off Mike.

She watched as Mike knelt down and lifted up the seven-year-old black boy and softly judo-flipped him over his shoulder onto the couch next to an Asian girl.

She certainly hadn't expected this.

"Hey!" one of the kids yelled. "Check it out!"

On the TV screen, Emily and Mike were on the

sidewalk in front of the Bronx building. The coverage of the kidnapping had already begun.

The children all started clapping. One of the tween girls put her pinkies in her mouth and whistled like a doorman hailing a taxi. Emily chuckled as she watched Bennett take an elaborate bow.

"Thank you, everyone. No autographs, please. Enough fame for now, it's time to eat!"

And the dinner, Emily thought as they finally sat, looked incredible. One of the hugest dining room tables she'd ever seen, and set with china, no less. How did they manage that? Looking at the faces of the kids finding their seats, she thought of herself and Olivia eating Lean Cuisines at the kitchen island in her silent town house. Could this be more different?

They all folded their hands together and closed their eyes as the priest led them in saying grace.

"Bless us, O Lord, and these, Thy gifts, which we are about to receive from Thy bounty through Christ our Lord, amen," the sweet old man said. "Now pass the gravy!"

She didn't just see that, did she? The setting looked like a lost cover of *The Saturday Evening Post,* only it was real. The only time she ever had a home-cooked meal like this was on Thanksgiving at her dad's house.

The last thing Emily had expected when she was called on special assignment this afternoon was that she'd be eating dinner with some crazy, enormous, happy family. She couldn't wait to call her daughter and tell her all about them.

She shook her head as she caught Mike's eye at the head of the table.

"And a cat, too?" she said.

"Ah, he's just another loafer," Mike said. "Like the priest."

Chapter 18

AFTER WE ATE, all the kids lined up to say good night to Emily.

"It was indeed a pleasure to meet you," Trent said, still hamming it up. "And good night, Father. Do sleep well."

"Oh," I said, tickling him hard enough to make him squeal. "Do sleep well yourself, Sir Hamlet."

When we were finally alone, I poured Emily the last of the wine and gave her the short version of my life story. I told her about Maeve, my wife. How we'd adopted our kids, one by one, until we turned around one day and saw that we had ten. I even told her how my wife had passed away. How Mary Catherine and Seamus and I struggled to keep the wheels from falling off.

"But enough about me," I said, getting that off my chest. "Fair's fair. It's time for you to give me the vitals on Emily Parker."

"There's not much. I have one daughter. Olivia," she said, taking a picture out of her bag.

"A cutie," I said, leaning in close to Emily to see the picture. *Like her mother,* I almost said. It was amazing how comfortable this was starting to feel.

"How old is she?" I said instead.

"Four."

"The only age we don't have in this house," I said. "What are the odds?"

Mary Catherine came in with two plates and caught us laughing.

"Mary, that isn't what I think it is, is it? Apple pie?" Emily said.

Mary Catherine dropped the plates loudly on the table.

"I left the stove on," she said, quickly turning around. "*Will* that be all tonight, Mr. Bennett?"

"Sure... that's fine, Mary," I said, a little confused.

When the kitchen door closed, I lifted the picture of Olivia off the table.

"So, where's Olivia's dad?" I said. I put the picture down. *Wow, did I just say that out loud? Real subtle there, Mike.* "I'm sorry. You don't have to answer that."

"No, it's okay. Olivia's dad is in, um, California. We've been divorced two years now. We met in the air force. John was a little rough around the edges, but he was loving and funny and a brilliant natural mechanic. I always thought of him as the impulsive yin to my everything-in-its-place yang.

"In the beginning, everything was fine. John ran the service department of the Bethesda Mercedes dealership as I got promoted up through the ranks of the Bureau. It was hectic, of course, juggling two jobs and then Olivia, but we were a team, a real family. Then, two days after Olivia's second birthday, John announced he needed to redefine himself.

"First came the tats and the piercings, and then finally, without my knowledge, the purchase of a body shop in California with most of our joint savings."

"Ouch," I said.

"Yeah, *ouch* is the word. JonJon's Rods does custom hot rods for all the stars now, GTOs, Shelby Cobras. California's actually been really good for him."

"And really, really shitty for you and your daughter," I said.

Emily finished her wine and placed the glass carefully on the tablecloth in front of her.

"I should get going before you have to roll me out of here, Mike. I can't tell you what a nice time I had.

Your kids are even more incredible than that meal was. You're a lucky man."

"I'll get you a taxi," I said, standing.

The dining room table was cleared by the time I got back upstairs. I found Mary Catherine in the kitchen, banging dishes into the machine.

"Mary Catherine, you didn't happen to see my slice of pie, did you?"

"Oh, sorry. I tossed it," she said without turning around. "I thought you were done."

She wiped her hands on a dish towel and opened the back door, heading to her room on our prewar's top floor.

"Good night, now," she said, slamming the door behind her.

Chrissy came into the kitchen then in her pajamas as I was wrapping my mind around what had just occurred.

"Daddy, Shawna says that Emily Parker is your new girlfriend. Is that true?" Chrissy said.

Oh, I thought, staring at the just-slammed door. Okay. Now I got it.

Like I said, men are dumb.

Part Two

FINAL EXAM

Chapter 19

CHELSEA SKINNER COULDN'T stop trembling. At first it was strictly because of fear, but after three hours of lying bound on a bone-numbingly cold stone floor, she felt like she was actually freezing to death.

The only other time she could remember being as cold was when she went skiing in Colorado for the first time, when she was six. Seeing her breath in the backyard of the house that her dad had just built, she'd made her mom crack up as she pretended to smoke an imaginary cigarette.

Chelsea began to cry through her chattering teeth. That was her problem right there, wasn't it? Always wanting to be older, always having to push it. Why couldn't she just be satisfied? It was as if there were a hole inside her, and no matter what she tried to fill it with—clothes, food, friends, drugs, boys—there was always just a little itty-bitty space left that kept her from feeling like a whole person. She practically deserved this. It was bound to happen. It was—

Stop! she commanded herself. *You stop that right now!*

She'd been abducted, and she was getting down on herself? Blaming herself? That had to stop yesterday. This wasn't therapy. This wasn't a confidence-building activity at Big Country, the wilderness rehab camp that her parents had sent her to last summer to "get her rear in gear," as her dad had so cornily put it.

This was real.

Fact: Someone had knocked her out in front of her house as she was coming back from a night of dancing.

Fact: Someone had removed her jeans and T-shirt, and she was now in her bra and underwear.

Fact: Her hands and feet were bound with giant plastic twist-tie strips, and she was being held against her will in what felt like a crypt.

All the facts were bizarre, horrible when you got right down to it, but very, very real. She suddenly remembered something that Lance, her Big Country eco-psychologist, had kept stressing. *You make your own reality.*

At the time, she'd thought it was the stupidest thing she'd ever heard, but now, as she considered it, maybe this was what he meant. When you were in a very bad situation, you could either feel sorry for yourself or you could—

Chelsea stilled herself as the lights went on. The door to the dilapidated room she was locked in creaked open. The saliva in her mouth evaporated.

At the threshold stood a man wearing a suit and a ski mask.

This isn't happening, she thought as the man stepped in and knelt down beside her.

"Hey, Chels," the man said in a polished voice. Then he head-butted her in the face and the world dimmed.

She gained consciousness to a zipping sound. The man in the ski mask was tightening the last of the straps of the appliance hand truck that she was now lashed to. He rolled her out of the room and bumped her up some steps and whirled her dizzily around a long, tiled corridor.

The room they entered had a low ceiling and a long stainless-steel counter that ran the length of one wall. She came to a clanking stop.

"I didn't—," Chelsea said, shaking now. "I d-d-didn't do anything."

"Exactly," her abductor said from behind her. "Maybe you should have. Have you considered that? Have you considered what you have failed to do?"

As she watched, the man went over to the sink. He lifted an orange five-gallon Home Depot bucket from underneath it and opened the tap.

"Now, I want you to take a little test," he said as he filled the bucket. "The subject is water. Did you know that one-point-one billion people worldwide lack access to fresh drinking water? That's a lot of folks, wouldn't you say? Now, my question is this: How much clean water does it take to wash your Abercrombie and Fitch T-shirt and Dolce and Gabbana jeans?"

I am having a nightmare, Chelsea thought, staring at the man as he turned off the tap and stepped back, holding the heavy bucket easily in his left hand.

I am Alice, and I have dropped down the rabbit hole and eaten the wrong slice of cake.

Chelsea finally lowered her eyes.

"I don't know," she said in an almost whisper.

Without warning, the man grasped the bottom of the bucket and swung it forward. The water that hit her full in the face was frigid. If she thought she was cold before, she was out of her mind. She was Arctic Sea–cold now. Deep space–cold.

"It takes forty gallons!" the man in the ski mask screamed. "In the villages of rural Cambodia and northern Uganda, two to three hundred people struggle daily to share one hand pump in order to get the water they need to survive. Families die for water. The only time you give it the foggiest thought is when a waiter asks you if you want yours sparkling or not!

"Now, question number two: How many thousands of children die every day throughout our world from water-related illnesses, like cholera, dysentery, and hepatitis?"

Chelsea was no longer listening. She was too cold to hear, to think. It was like a glacier was moving through her body now, petrifying her muscles and tendons and bones. It would reach her heart soon, she thought, and the cold would make it seize up like a frozen engine.

The man went back to the sink with the bucket. He began whistling the theme from final *Jeopardy!* as he squealed open the tap again.

Chapter 20

A MIGRAINE HEADACHE woke Emily Parker at the ungodly hour of six a.m. Now that's what I call a wake-up call, she thought, wincing as she sat up. She'd been suffering from migraines on and off ever since she was in college. The pulsating, stabbing sensation was always in the same place, above her left eye, as if something were trying to dig its way out of her skull with an ice pick.

Sometimes it was so bad, it made her vomit. Sometimes, for some inexplicable reason, it made her extremely thirsty. Before he left, her New Age husband, John, had suggested that it was the price for her investigative skill, the price for her ability to make intuitive leaps that saved people's lives.

Or maybe it was the stress brought on by my no-good husband, she wished she could tell him now.

She found her bag and fished out an Imitrex, her headache prescription. Swallowing it dry, she saw a flashing image of Jacob Dunning dead in the South Bronx boiler room.

What was she still doing here? she thought. Her boss told her to hang tight up in New York, at least until the results from the medical examiner were in, but she wasn't sure. Thirty-five was definitely too old for this shit in the Bureau's Behavioral Analysis Unit. She found herself missing her cozy beige cubicle and cinder-block walls. Or maybe she should get out altogether and try to get a teaching job. Something that coincided with Olivia's schedule. Give some fresh, young world beater the chance to go after these monsters, deal with these poor families.

She was shaking another Imitrex into her palm when her cell went off.

"Hey, it's Mike," Bennett said. "Sorry to wake you up."

She found herself smiling. His calm voice was like a lifeboat against the nauseating waves of tightness in her skull. She remembered dinner, his crazy kids. At least that had been fun.

"Tell me something good, Mike," she said. "The media coverage jogged someone's memory?"

"I wish," he said. "I just got off the phone with my boss. Looks like we got another missing kid. Her name is Chelsea Skinner. She's seventeen, and her father is the president of the New York Stock Exchange. Friends let her out of a cab on the corner of her street early this morning, but she never made it home."

"Already? My God! Even for a serial, that's unbelievably fast to do it again," Emily said. "Should we head to the family's residence?"

"No," Bennett said. "Schultz and Ramirez are already on their way. Our presence has actually been requested at the task force meeting they're putting together down at headquarters. I'll pick you up at eight-thirty so we can get our game faces on. You like lox on your bagel? I don't think the Jewish deli I go to has grits, but I can ask. What are grits, anyway?"

"Tell me, Mike," Emily said with a smile. "Are all New York cops wiseasses twenty-four/seven?"

"Just the good-looking ones with double-digit kids," Bennett said. "See you in a few hours, Agent Parker."

Chapter 21

THE TASK FORCE meeting was at a brand-new section of One Police Plaza's tenth floor. They must have pulled out all the stops with Homeland Security money, because it looked like a war room out of Hollywood.

There were brand-new flat-panel monitors everywhere, state-of-the-art telephone and radio com hookups, and huge PowerPoint screens covering one of the large space's long walls. You could still smell the chemicals in the new carpet. Or maybe that was just the shoe polish that glossed the expensive wingtips of all the high-powered attendants.

The mayor was back early, I noticed, with our old pal Georgina Hottinger hovering around him like a scavenger fish around a shark. They were busy conferring with police commissioner Daly and his contingent of white-uniform-shirted chiefs. There was even a group of healthy-looking guys with executive hair whom I could only assume were colleagues of Emily's.

Emily went over to powwow with the other Fibbies a moment after we entered. I made myself busy by taking out my cell phone and checking for any updates.

Right before the festivities were about to begin, Emily returned to where I was sitting double-fisted with coffees.

"I put a rush on the lab down in Washington for the ashes on Jacob's forehead. The eggheads are waiting with bated breath," she said.

"Good," I said. "I heard back about the phone numbers. It looks like our guy hired illegals to buy the phones in cash from the three different stores. Also, Verizon Wireless pinpointed where his calls were made from. The first came back on the West Side Highway and the second one from the FDR Drive. Apparently, he was on the move the whole time he was talking to us."

Ten minutes later, Emily and I went to the front of the room and briefed everyone about Jacob Dunning.

"Sometime in the early-morning hours of Saturday the twenty-first of February, Jacob Dunning was abducted outdoors by an unknown subject. The subject contacted the family on Sunday. A second call was made a few hours later, during which the abductor requested to speak to us.

"Proceeding by the abductor's instruction to two-five-oh Briggs Avenue, a high-crime area of the Bronx, we found Jacob in the basement, shot once in the head with a three-eighty-caliber bullet. The body was found in a child's school desk in front of a blackboard, indicating a high level of scene staging. There was what appeared to be a cross or an *X* made probably of ashes on the victim's forehead. No foreign DNA, latent prints, or ballistic casings were found."

I nodded to Emily.

"In terms of motive, there's no clear indication as of yet," she said. "No monetary demands were made. We're not sure if the kidnapper was about to ask for money but then didn't because of police interference. A question-and-answer sequence between the abductor and the victim does seem to suggest some vague political motives.

"Preliminary voice analysis seems to indicate that the subject is male, over the age of thirty-five, and highly educated. The subject also seems to have known many intimate details about the victim and his family, so some connection to the Dunnings by the suspect remains a distinct possibility. That's all we have."

Chief Fleming stood.

"For those of you who don't already know, early this morning, a seventeen-year-old Riverdale resident by the name of Chelsea Skinner was reported missing. Her father, Harold Skinner, is the president of the New York Stock Exchange. Though there's been no contact from anyone yet, we're treating this as an abduction by the same person until further notice."

There was a lot of shocked head shaking as we returned to our seats. And even more grumbling. Right now, we had no good leads, just about the worst-case scenario for the department in a high-profile media case.

I wasn't surprised at all when Georgina Hottinger sat herself next to us a few minutes later. Giving her useless two cents seemed to be her favorite hobby.

"There are to be no information leaks from this task force, and I mean none. Anyone who is thinking of calling their hook at whatever media outlet better think again if they value their jobs. The last thing we need is some media circus."

She turned and stared directly at Emily.

"Am I coming in loud and clear?" she said.

"Not that clear," Emily said with her charming southern smile. "But definitely loud."

Chapter 22

OVER THE NEXT hour, a Major Case management setup was hashed out. A command group of all the chiefs would be situated at One PP along with the intelligence coordinators who would be in charge of collecting, processing, analyzing, and disseminating all the different leads and breaks in the case. A rapid-start operations group along with a separate investigative group was put on call to be sent to pertinent crime scenes and victim residences.

Emily and I, as the lead investigative coordinators, headed directly out to the Skinners' residence in the Riverdale section of the Bronx. We didn't have to be told twice to get away from all that brass.

My phone rang as we got on the West Side Highway.

"Bennett here."

"Bennett here, too, Detective," Seamus said. "I wanted to go over the plans for you-know-who's you-know-what."

He was talking about Mary Catherine. Her birthday was coming up on Wednesday, and we were planning a big surprise bash. I shook my head. I'd better come up with something good. With the funny way she was acting lately, this was pretty much going to have to be the social event of the year or I was doomed.

"I'm busy right this second," I said. "I'll have to call you back."

"Oh, I get it. You're with her right now, are ya?" Seamus said in a conspiratorial tone. "Oh, she's a cute one, all right. I'd have a crush on her, too, if I was your age. Give me a note, and I'll pass it to her. You know you want to."

I hung up on him.

"Who was that?" Emily said.

"Wrong number," I mumbled.

Emily shook her head at me with a smile.

"I've been meaning to ask you. How do you do it?" she said. "Great cop. Great dad. Head screwed on straight. How does that happen with ten kids? Oh, and a cat. Now that's just showing off, don't you think?"

I laughed as I gunned it north toward the Bronx.

"You see right through me," I said. "I rent the cat for atmosphere."

Chapter 23

THE SKINNERS' HOUSE was on Independence Avenue about a half mile west of the Henry Hudson Parkway near Wave Hill. A stunning view of the Hudson River rolled silently behind the ivy-draped rambling Tudor.

There was a genteel country air about the landscaped neighborhood. Getting out of the car, I thought about how nice it would be to have a backyard. I imagined the peace and quiet as I sat on warm grass with a cold drink. More like fantasized. Within the confines of New York City, genteel country airs with river views usually go for about eight figures.

We met Schultz and Ramirez in the horseshoe-shaped gravel drive.

"Last night around ten, Chelsea snuck out of her house to party downtown with a couple of girlfriends," Ramirez said, reading his notes. "They said they let her out of a cab here on the corner of West Two Hundred and Fifty-fourth at around two-thirty. They didn't want to drop her right in front of the house because they didn't want to wake up her parents. Her mom found Chelsea's bag with her cell phone in it on the driveway just before six. He must have been waiting for her. Nobody saw any cars or people. Neighbors didn't hear a thing."

"Already checked out the Skinners," Schultz said. "Parents are clean, but Chelsea got a desk-appearance ticket for drinking on the subway about a year ago. Chelsea, apparently, is a bit of a handful."

I counted four luxury cars parked in the Skinners' driveway as we walked toward the portico. A tall, upset-looking man in a pinstripe suit pulled open the door as we were about to ring the bell.

"Well, have you heard anything?" he said, staring at my shield. "Have you found Chelsea? I want answers."

"Are you Harold Skinner?" I said.

"No, I'm not. Mr. Skinner is busy dying of grief that his daughter has been taken from him."

A plump middle-aged woman appeared behind him.

"Mark," she said to the man. "You're my brother and I love you, but would you, please, just for one second, do me a favor and stop?

"I'm Rachael Skinner," she said, shaking my hand. "Please come in."

About a dozen of Chelsea's extended family were sitting in the dead silent living room. They were red-eyed and shattered-looking, like mourners at a wake. Another tight-knit family was in agony this morning.

"Is Mr. Skinner around?" I said. "We're going to have to speak to him as well."

"I'm sorry," Mrs. Skinner said. "He's resting right now. Sedated, actually. The family physician left a few minutes before you arrived. Tell me something, if you would, Detective. I heard that the other boy who was taken was found with ashes on his forehead. That's a Catholic thing, isn't it, with the ashes? We're Jewish. What do ashes signify?"

How did she know about that? I thought. We'd kept that out of the media coverage. Someone in the task force must have spilled it. My money was on Deputy Mayor Hottinger. So much for plugging all the leaks.

"It's a sign of willingness for Catholics to repent for their sins," I said. "In addition to abstaining from indulgences like smoking or drinking and eating meat on Friday, it's a way to symbolically share Christ's sacrifice during Lent."

"I see. Then this person, the kidnapper, is Catholic?"

"We don't know what he is," I told the poor woman truthfully. "We don't even know that Chelsea's been kidnapped. Don't assume the worst, ma'am. Let's take things one at a time."

Chapter 24

THERE WAS A family-photo wall in the hallway leading to the kitchen. Chelsea was a beautiful black-haired girl with striking light blue, almost gray, eyes. In the latest picture, she was wearing a hoodie with *Lifeguard* written across the front.

"Your daughter's beautiful," Emily said as Mrs. Skinner guided us to a large, bright kitchen table.

"Chelsea had a brain tumor when she was six, a medulloblastoma on her brain stem," the kind woman said quietly as she poured us coffee. "She completely beat it. The operations. The chemo. She's a fighter. This is nothing compared to that. She'll get out of this. I know she will."

I wished I could have shared Mrs. Skinner's startling conviction.

Some PD TARU guys arrived and got up on the Skinners' wall phones and cell phones. An FBI tech from the New York office showed up as well and installed some e-mail–tracing software, in case our guy decided to switch tactics.

Mrs. Skinner showed us Chelsea's room on the third floor. It had a huge, sloping beamed ceiling and a little balcony that overlooked the garden and the covered in-ground pool. It was sleek with modern furniture. It looked more like a rich thirty-five-year-old's room than a teenager's. Jacob's room by comparison looked unsophisticated, childish.

There had to be a link between Chelsea and Jacob. They were both only children, both rich. We'd learned that Chelsea attended Fieldston, a nearby expensive private school that was close to Horace Mann, where Jacob had gone to high school. Had they known each other? Maybe there was a teacher who had worked at both places. Was that the connection?

One thing I was sure of, this guy was definitely not picking these kids out of a hat.

After Mrs. Skinner left, Emily pulled on a pair of rubber gloves and got on the kid's laptop. Chelsea's home page was her MySpace page.

Over Emily's shoulder I read parts of Chelsea's blog. Some of what she was saying was pretty out there. Sexual boastings. Violent fantasies. I was shocked to see that there were some fairly explicit photos of her.

"Is this what kids are up to now?" Emily said.

I shook my head alongside her as a photo of Chelsea with mascara-thick eyelashes leered from the screen. Was this what I would have to look forward to when my daughter Julia turned seventeen in three years?

"God, I hope not," I said. "Note to self: Become Mennonite and save money for house in the middle of nowhere. I have ten kids. We could learn to farm, right? Get back to Mother Earth, reduce our carbon footprint, and build character all at the same time."

"Don't forget the cat," Emily said.

"Socky. Right," I said. "He could herd the cows."

Chapter 25

I WAS COMING out of Chelsea's room when the phone rang. But it wasn't the Skinners' phone. It was mine.

"Mike, hello. How'd you sleep? Well, I hope?"

Son of a bitch! I stopped in midstride, adrenaline jolting through me like live wire. It was him! The sly bastard was calling me instead of the house.

"Fine," I said, ungluing myself from the carpet and racing downstairs into the study, where we were set up. I found the department tech and pointed excitedly at my phone. He retrieved a handheld voice recorder from a laptop bag and handed it to me. I held it by my phone's earpiece.

"I'm glad you called back," I said. "Where are you? Maybe we could talk in person?"

"Maybe," he said. "But then again, maybe not, Mike. How do you like the Skinners' place? Exquisite, wouldn't you say?"

What? He knew I was here? Or was he just guessing? Was he watching the place?

"And that view," he continued. "The grandeur of the mighty river beneath those austere crags. Truly to die for, if you'll excuse the term. Thomas Cole himself could hardly have done it justice, wouldn't you agree? But what am I doing, dropping such names to a policeman? Thomas Cole was a painter, you see. He started the Hudson River School."

"Was Frederic Edwin Church a Hudson River School guy?" I said, to keep him talking.

"Why, yes, he was, Mike. You know your art history. Where did you go to school?"

The police academy, scumbag, I felt like saying to him.

"Manhattan College," I said instead.

"Never heard of it," the kidnapper said.

"Well, it's pretty small," I said. "Could we speak to Chelsea? We're ready to give you what you want if you'd only tell us."

Then he said the words I was dreading.

"If that's the case, then listen closely," he said. "I want you to come and get it. I want you to come and get little Chels and bring her back to Mumsy. You know the drill. Get in a car. Ten minutes. You can bring your pretty little FBI friend, too, if you like."

Chapter 26

THE CIRCLE LINE tour boat was coming through the Amtrak swing bridge down on the Harlem River as we raced across the Henry Hudson Bridge.

And if you look up, ladies and gents, I thought, emergency lights blazing through the lower level's E-Z Pass lane, *you'll see an authentic, stressed-out New York City cop about to break the sound barrier.*

I clicked the siren to full auto as we blasted through the Manhattan-side tolls at a stomach-churning seventy.

We'd just been told Chelsea was in Harlem. I couldn't lose another kid. If there was any possible way to get to her before it was too late, I was going to do it.

"Where are you now?" the kidnapper said into the ear of my hands-free headset. Again, he'd insisted on guiding me street by street. My own personal insane OnStar operator.

"On the Manhattan side of the Henry Hudson Bridge," I said.

"Did you know that it was built by Robert Moses back in the thirties using New Deal labor?" he said. "In twenty years, Moses managed to build most of New York City's major bridges, parkways, and public beaches. The Twin Towers were knocked down almost ten years ago, and it's still just a pit. Our civilization is winding down, Mike. It's obvious. So's our planet. Take a fork out of the drawer and turn off the oven timer. This place is done."

"Hello? Hello? I think the signal's breaking up," I said as I whipped off the headset to clear the sweat and bull crap out of my ears. Beside me, Emily was working two radios and her cell phone as we gunned it south. I cupped my cell's microphone.

"How are we looking?" I whispered.

Besides Aviation and the Emergency Service Unit backing us up, the phone company was on board now, actively working on a trace.

"Verizon's still trying to triangulate," Emily said. "Nothing so far."

As I drove, I racked my brain to come up with a way to try to throw the kidnapper off balance, turn the tables on him. He was in charge, and what was worse from the smug tone of his voice, it sounded like he knew it.

"Are you there?" he was saying angrily when I patched back in.

"Hello? Hello?" I said. "The signal seems to be back now."

"The signal, huh? I believe you, Mike. Almost. Now take the George Washington Bridge exit."

Shit, I thought. That exit was already blowing past on my left. I spun the wheel, mercilessly mowing down a family of construction traffic cones on the exit's shoulder. We missed a head-on with a construction light cart by a few millimeters as I just made it back into the lane.

"Can you hear me now?" the kidnapper said. "Head over to Broadway, if it's not too much trouble."

Chapter 27

I FOLLOWED THE kidnapper's instructions through Washington Heights and on deeper into Harlem. As we turned off Broadway at St. Nicholas Avenue, we passed a series of enormous housing projects that were as stark and depressing as warehouses in an industrial plant.

Bulletproof windows began to appear on the corner delis and Chinese takeouts. It looked a lot like the section of the Bronx where we'd found Jacob Dunning.

I was on another magical misery tour of the inner city, complete with constant narration.

"Take a good look around, Mike," the kidnapper said. "Remember the War on Poverty? Poverty won.

African Americans and Latino immigrants were lured into the cities because of jobs, and then the jobs moved away with all the white people. The racial and economic inequality that still exists in this country makes me physically sick sometimes.

"It's not just here, either. Look at places like Newark, Pittsburgh, St. Louis. It's the twenty-first century, and still there's a lack of decent employment and no shortage of discrimination toward people of color."

"Where to now?" I said.

"You're getting warm. Make a left onto One Hundred and Forty-first, a left onto Bradhurst, and a right onto One Hundred and Forty-second," the kidnapper said.

At 142nd, a single, leaning brownstone stood on the corner of a mostly rubble-filled lot. I slowed, scanning its surrounding weeds. I spotted a diaper, a mattress, and a rusty shopping cart but, thankfully, no Chelsea.

"Go to two-eight-six. That's where she is, Mike. Time for me to go. Tell Mom I said hi," he said and hung up.

I rapidly scanned the buildings and screeched to a stop in front of the address. I jumped out of the car and stared up at the onion-shaped dome above the three-story building in front of me.

"It's a mosque," I radioed our backup. "I repeat.

We're at two-eight-six One Hundred and Forty-second Street. It's on the north side of the street. We can't wait. We're going in the front."

We opened a pair of elaborate doors and rushed into a large, shabby, definitely unchic lobby. It looked like the mosque had been converted from an old movie theater.

"Hello?" I called as we entered an open area where the seats had once been. There were windows in its walls now, and the floor was covered in Oriental rugs. It must be the prayer room, I figured. The light-filled space was divided in half by a large lace screen, and one of the walls was covered in elaborate tile.

A stocky black man wearing a bright green, red, and yellow kufi on his head appeared in a doorway at the other end of the room. He hurried over, shock and anger in his face.

"Who are you? What are you doing here? You're not allowed in here. Your shoes! You can't wear shoes here in the mussalah. Are you crazy? Can't you see this is a holy place?"

I showed him my shield.

"I'm with the police department. We're looking for a girl who was—"

That's when the Muslim man grabbed me violently by the lapels of my suit jacket.

"I don't care who you are," he cried, dragging me toward the door. "This is a sacrilege! Get out of here now! You have no right to do this!"

As we were busy struggling, I remembered the Harlem mosque incident in the seventies in which an NYPD cop had been killed. A police community conflict was all we needed now in the middle of a kidnapping.

A moment later, the muscular man suddenly fell to his side. Emily had tripped him somehow and now had her knee in his back as she ratcheted her cuffs onto his wrists. I helped her pull the hysterical man to his feet.

"Sir," Emily said. "Please calm yourself. We're sorry about the shoe mistake. We were unaware and apologize. We are law enforcement officers looking for a kidnapped girl. We were told she was here. Please help us. A young girl's life is at stake."

"I see," he said. "I'm Yassin Ali, the imam here. I lost my temper. Of course, I'll do anything to help."

Emily undid his cuffs, and he guided us back out into the foyer.

"You say a girl is being held here?" he said, staring at us in disbelief. "But that's impossible. There hasn't been anyone here since morning prayer. What's this girl's name? Is she a member of the congregation?"

I showed him Chelsea's picture.

"A white girl?" he said, perplexed. "No. There's no way. There must be a mistake."

"Has anything out of the ordinary occurred today? Anything that might direct us to where this girl could be?" I said. "Any deliveries or—?"

"No." Then something flashed in his eyes.

"Actually, yes. When I came in, I heard a loud noise from the side of the building, where my office is. There's an alley between us and the construction site next door. I thought maybe one of the workers had dumped some debris again, but when I looked out, there was nothing."

"Please show us," Emily said. "We don't have a moment to waste."

Chapter 28

THE SIDE ALLEY Yassin showed us was appalling. Water—from a busted sewage line, judging by its stench—cascaded down the brick wall of the building under construction next door. A faded blue tarp flapped from a hole on its third floor.

You knew you were in a bad section of Manhattan when even the real-estate flippers had abandoned ship.

The piles of debris in the dim alley looked like something out of a photography book about the Great Depression. I rushed ahead, wishing we'd brought a pair of wading boots as I slogged over garbage bags, old bricks, the rusted door of a car.

I was coming back from the rear of the alley when I almost tripped over a fridge discarded on its back with the door still attached. By law, supers were supposed to remove the doors because of the notorious suffocation death-trap threat to curious kids.

My breath caught as a thought suddenly occurred to me.

I flipped up the fridge's freezer door with the heel of my shoe.

Something went loose in my chest as I stared down.

I didn't want to be seeing what I was seeing, yet I had to drag my eyes away. Then I reeled back to the alley's fence behind me. With a shaking hand held over my mouth, I stood staring at the broken glass glittering in the rubble-strewn field beyond the alley. A train creaked and clattered in the distance. The wind played with a plastic bag.

I went back only when Emily got to the spot. We stood beside the open fridge, solemn and silent like mourners beside a strange white casket.

From inside, Chelsea Skinner stared back at us.

Her neck must have been broken when she'd been crammed in, because her body was twisted, facing the ground. It looked like her legs had been broken as well in order to fit her inside.

There was a bullet hole in the top of her head, and she had a cross made of ashes on her forehead.

Emily placed her gloved hand on the dead girl's cheek.

"I'm going to catch the man who did this to you," she promised the girl as she took out her phone.

Chapter 29

THE SUBWOOFER THUMPING of the low-flying PD chopper seemed to echo through my raging blood as I left Emily and threaded the narrow alley back to the sidewalk.

I stared at the line of decrepit three- and four-story brick town houses across the street. The ground floors of many of the buildings bore the closed steel shutters of abandoned stores, but I could see curtains and blinds in many of the upstairs windows that faced the alley. Somebody must have seen something.

A crowd had gathered around the just-arrived Emergency Service Unit truck, which was parked in front of the mosque. I could see Lieutenant Montana through the windshield, working the radio, calling for backup. Around the truck were many mosque-goers, men in kufis and some women wearing hijab head scarves. But others—local non-Muslim street folk looking for some stimulation—also seemed to be arriving by the minute.

I took out a picture of Chelsea as I walked over to the throng of people. "This girl was found dead in the alley back there," I announced, holding it up. "Did anyone see anything this morning?"

"Oh, a white girl. That's what all the fuss is about. Figures," said a pudgy young woman, laughing between bites of her takeout.

"Word," said a large man in cornrows beside her. "Why you cops messing around this mosque for? These are God-fearin' people. This is harassment. Religious *and* racial discrimination. We don't know anything about any white girl!"

From the way the large man stood, half turned, unconsciously shielding his right side, I would have bet my paycheck that he was carrying under his XXL Giants jersey. I wanted to bust him right there and then. Make the wiseass the recipient of the anger that was still reeling through me. I almost didn't care that it would probably incite the rest of the gathering crowd.

I exhaled a long breath and let it go as a couple of

Twenty-fifth Precinct radio cars turned the corner a moment later.

I was heading back toward the crime scene when I heard a window slam across the street. Behind the pane of dusty glass in one of the town houses' second-story windows, a thin, middle-aged black woman stared down at me. She made extended, knowing eye contact with me and nodded before fading back further into her apartment.

She wanted to talk, but not in front of the neighborhood. *Please, let this be a lead,* I prayed as I went to get Emily.

I left a couple of uniforms to cordon off the alley and took Emily with me across the street. The town house's inner door's lock buzzed as we entered the foyer. As we reached the top of the narrow stairwell, a door cracked open down the hallway. The woman whom I'd seen in the window put her finger to her lips and motioned us silently inside.

The apartment was immaculate. The furniture was arranged tastefully on polished hardwood floors, and there was a granite island in the stainless-steel kitchen. Through an open bathroom doorway, I spotted a nurse's flowered uniform blouse hanging on the shower curtain rod.

The woman introduced herself as Mrs. Price, and

I showed her Chelsea's picture as we stepped into the living room.

"This girl's body was found dumped across the street," I said, keeping my voice down.

The woman tsked loudly as she stared at the photo.

"Another dead child," she said in a lilting Caribbean accent. "I'd say dis world has gone damn crazy, but I don't remember a time when it wasn't."

"Is there some information you could share with us, Mrs. Price?" Emily prompted. "This probably happened right after the call-to-prayer speakers went off at five."

"Oh, I know dose damn speakers," she said. "Dey shouldn't be allowed to do dat. Religion or not, dat's noise pollution. I called three-one-one a hundred times, but do you tink anytin happen? Tink again."

"Did you *see* anything?" Emily said.

"No," she said. "But you talk to dat Big Ice. He's de local drug dealer."

"The loud guy with the cornrows?" I said.

She pursed her lips as she nodded.

"Big Devil, I say he is. Making dis block a livin hell for all de decent folks with jobs, tryin to raise families. Big Ice's people are out all morning early on dat corner and stay out to all hours de next mornin.

If anytin happened on dis block, dey seen it, sure. He tinks he so slick, runnin tings from dat clothes store round de corner while his runners and such do his biddin."

"What's the name of the store?" I said.

"Ener-G Boutique. Sells all dat hip-hop nonsense clothes. It's right on de corner."

"You're a good person, ma'am," I said, putting the picture away. "Speaking up is a courageous thing."

"You tell dat beautiful young girl's mother I'm sorry for her loss," the thin woman said as we headed back to the door. "I raised three sons on dis block by de skin of my teeth. If dey were taken from me like dat, I don't know what I'd do."

Chapter 30

THE ENER-G BOUTIQUE was right where our witness said it would be. I thought it was going to be a fly-by-night front sort of place, but it actually seemed legit. In the window were name-brand clothes from the Wu-Tang Clan, Phat Farm, Sean John, G-Unit, FUBU. They apparently sold footwear, too, to judge from the neon Timberland and Nike signs on the plate-glass door.

The clerk, plucking her eyebrows behind the counter, didn't have a chance to say, "Can I help you?" by the time Emily and I, plus a couple of ESU SWAT cops, had crossed the store with our guns drawn. Big Ice was sitting on the shoe department's try-on bench, slipping on a pair of Nike Dunks, when we approached him.

"Yeah?" he said testily, looking up at us.

There were two cell phones beside him and a plastic Ener-G bag under the bench. Inside the bag, a chrome-plated automatic was plainly visible.

"I wouldn't move if I were you," I said as I knelt and lifted the bag. The gun was a Browning Hi Power 9-millimeter. "You have a license for this?" I said, showing it to him.

"Oh, that ain't *my* bag, Officer. Somebody else must have left it there. I just came in here to get me some new walkers."

There was a shoebox in the bag as well. I upended it onto the floor. A plastic bag holding a dozen tightly bound bundles of twenties bounced off the beige carpet.

"Then I take it this money isn't yours either. Or anything else I'm going to find when I tear this place apart."

"Oh, I get it," Big Ice said, looking from me to each of the cops surrounding him. "You gonna try and pin that girl on me. Some white girl dies, so let's blame the big black man. How original. This is bullshit."

Big Ice was right. What we were doing was not

ordinary police procedure by any stretch. I didn't care. I was past the point of doing this thing by the book. I didn't have time to listen to a thousand "I didn't see nothing"s. I was sick of looking at dead kids.

"Toss me my cellie so I can speed-dial my lawyer," Big Ice said, yawning casually. "I got that white boy on retainer. He's going to blow your inadmissible illegal-ass search the fuck up."

"Maybe," I said. "But Clarence-goddamn-Darrow isn't going to be able to get you back this shoebox full of twenties."

Big Ice suddenly looked at me as if I'd grown another head.

"Oh," he said, smiling. "You wanna play *Deal or No Deal*. Why didn't you just say so instead of bullin' in here, getting my lady all up in a dander? You come to the right place. What can I do for you?"

"I know you or your people are out on that corner early," I said. "That girl didn't fall from the sky. She was dumped there. You help me with some information about it, I'm going to let you get back to your shoe shopping. Might even leave this bag where that poor soul left it."

"With the piece in it?" Big Ice said hopefully.

"Nah, I'm going to have to turn this gun in to the lost and found," I said.

He took a loud breath as he considered. He finally nodded.

"Okay. I could make some calls," he said.

I tossed him one of his phones.

"What a guy," I said.

Chapter 31

WE STOOD AROUND as Big Ice made phone calls and left messages.

"Don't worry," he said, snapping his phone shut. "They know what'll happen to 'em if they don't call me back in less than ten minutes."

On the wall above a rack of Avirex leather jackets was a flat-screen TV tuned to the BET channel. Big Ice stood up laboriously, found the remote under the cash register, and changed it to CNBC. He stared at the screen intently as a bald white man in suspenders talked about IPOs.

"Damn, you think I'm bad?" Big Ice said. "How 'bout you go after some of those private-equity joints. Those homies buy multinational companies with

IOUs an' shit. I should try that at Micky D's. 'Hey, how much is that Big Mac? Three bucks? Okay, I'll take it, but instead of payin' you right now, you can have the five Stacy be owin' me whenever.' They wouldn't be lovin' that shit, would they? But you times that scam by a couple of billion, you get a hospital named after you. Now how's that work?"

Emily rolled her eyes at him.

"You in the market?" she said.

Big turned and stared at her.

"I look like someone who's risk-averse to you, shorty? Course, I'm in. I be workin' my S-an'-P portfolio all the time, re-up all those sweet dividends. You think them Knicks floor seats I got come cheap? You want, I could put you together with my broker," he said with a wink.

"Would you?" Emily said sarcastically as one of Big's phones rang.

"Listen good, Snap," Big Ice said into it. "You out on the corner early this morning? Shut up and listen, fool. You didn't see anybody over by the mosque real early, did you?"

Big listened, nodding.

"What's up?" he said into his cell phone a few moments later. "What's up is some white girl was found dead in the alley, chump, and I don't want to get locked up."

He closed his phone.

"Talk to us," I said.

"Snap said around five-thirty he saw a white guy get out of a beat-ass yellow van. Reason why he noticed was business is slow that early, and he thought the guy must be a desperate customer. I like to stay out a little earlier and later than everyone else, customers be appreciatin' that kind of extra service."

"I'm sure they do," I said impatiently. "Go on."

"Well, Snap said this thin, mousy-looking dude with glasses and gray hair, wearing coveralls and wheeling a refrigerator, got out of the van. He figured it was a guy making an early delivery to the construction site or something. White guy came back with just the hand truck, got back in the van, made a U-turn, and took off."

I knew not to ask him if Mr. Snap had taken down a plate number. It wasn't much, but we had something finally.

"That help you?" Big Ice said, smiling as he rubbed his dinner plate–size palms together.

I dropped the plastic bag of drug money on the counter.

"Don't invest it all in one index," Emily called back as we left.

Chapter 32

THE STREET CROWD seemed somewhat calmer when we arrived back at the mosque. Imam Yassin had come out on the sidewalk and was speaking to his flock in a soothing voice.

I called back to the task force and passed on the information we'd gotten. I said the tip was anonymous to avoid further inconveniencing the NYPD's newest friends, Big Ice and Snap.

"Okay, I'll type up the DD-five for you and get it to the appropriate people," said Detective Kramer, the Major Case detective who'd been put in charge of the Intelligence Squad.

I was getting paperwork done for me? I thought as I hung up. I was starting to like this task force stuff.

I caught up to John Cleary, the Crime Scene Unit supervisor, who was walking toward the alley with a biohazard box.

"Turns out the suspect didn't dump the body into the fridge, John," I said. "This guy actually dumped the fridge with the body already in it."

"No shit?" Cleary said, removing his cell phone from where it was clipped to the collar of his Tyvek suit. "In that case, instead of dislodging the body here," he said, "we'll put the whole fridge onto a flatbed and do it at the lab."

Back in my unmarked car, I called Detective Ramirez, still at the Skinners' house, and broke the bad news. He let out a deep breath.

"That sucks," Ramirez said. "This poor woman. She doesn't deserve this. I'll let her know, Mike. I'd rather shoot myself in the kneecap, but I'll tell her."

Not wanting to hear the grieving that would soon follow, I hung up quickly.

"So, what do you think?" Parker said, getting back into the car.

"I think we should eat," I said. "I know the perfect place. It'll almost make you forget the past couple of hours."

Ten minutes later, we walked through the door of Sylvia's restaurant on Lenox Avenue a few blocks away.

"You're in luck," I said to Emily, pointing to the menu after we sat down in the cozy, incredible-smelling place. "Not only do they have grits, they have collard greens, too."

"Collard greens? Well, lordy me," Emily drawled, wafting an imaginary fan at herself. "I'll never be hungry again, though I definitely wouldn't have pegged you as a soul food aficionado, Mike."

"Don't get me wrong, Parker. I can put away a six-pack and potato with the best of me Irish brethren. It was my wife who introduced me to it. She was the foodie. Every Saturday, she'd con Seamus into watching the gang, and she'd take me to new places. We used to come to the jazz brunch they throw here on Saturday afternoons."

Over a couple of racks of Sylvia's fall-off-the-bone ribs, we went over the case.

"I think things are looking up a little," Emily said between bites. "The witness was horrible, but by allowing there to be one, at least it means our guy is human, capable of making mistakes. I wasn't sure there for a little while. But bringing the body in a fridge and then dumping the fridge? That's... bizarre, wouldn't you say? He's going to an awful lot of trouble."

"Yeah," I said, wiping my mouth with a napkin. "It's not just a job for this freak. It's an adventure."

"I keep asking myself *why* he's doing it," Emily continued. "Why bother pretending it's a kidnapping at all? He hasn't asked for any ransom. I mean, why even contact the families if you're just going to kill the vics?"

"Attention," I said. "Has to be. He's making this as dramatic as he can. Why do most of these psychopaths do this? They're inadequate in some fundamental way, yet have this grandiose ego. Look at Oswald. The Columbine fools. They can't be famous in a regular way, so they get attention by killing."

"But," Emily said, raising a barbecue-sauce-coated finger across the table, "you've spoken to this guy, Mike. He seems educated and very articulate. He doesn't strike me as inadequate."

I shrugged.

"Then he must be deformed or something, because no way is that staging and Q-and-A stuff a setup. Our cultured friend is getting his rocks off."

"You have a point there," Emily said.

I was shocked when the waitress came back around and Emily ordered a Jack Daniel's.

"What happened to the full-sugar Coke? You hear that rumbling sound? That's the sound of J. Edgar rolling over in his grave."

"What can I say, Mike? You've completely

corrupted me," Emily said with a wink. "They warned me about you New York cops. Stupid me. I should have listened."

When the check came, I tucked my credit card over the bill.

"Hold on. What are you doing?" Emily said, going into her purse. "We're splitting this. You're acting like this is a date."

"Am I?" I said, staring into her eyes as I handed the bill to the waitress.

She stared back for a couple of long, very pleasant moments. She blushed. No, actually that was me.

What the hell I was doing, I didn't know. My wife had been dead two years, and usually I felt unsettled when it came to new lady friends. Special Agent Emily Parker was different, I guess.

Or maybe I was just going crazy. That was probably it.

Chapter 33

IT WAS ALMOST nine p.m. when the end-of-day task force meeting ended, and an exhausted Emily Parker arrived back at her hotel. Six minutes after that, the top of her head hit the surface of the hotel's indoor lap pool with a satisfying smack.

There was nothing like that first, magical moment for her. Like she did in every new pool she was in, she plunged down into the cold serenity of the water until her hand passed across the pool's gritty bottom.

She sat Indian-style and closed her eyes. There were no worries down here. No aggravated bosses. No stresses. Certainly no dead children.

When she was growing up, her family had a pool in Virginia, and she'd spent practically every moment of every summer, from the time she was six until she turned ten, at the bottom of it pretending she was a mermaid. She'd close her eyes and put out her hand, waiting for it to be enveloped by her beloved merprince, who'd take her away to her lost kingdom.

When her lungs began to burn almost a minute later, Emily remembered that Chelsea Skinner had been a lifeguard.

She broke the surface and started her workout. Usually laps were enough to clear her head, but even after five, she couldn't help thinking about the case. Swimming the English Channel probably wouldn't have been enough to get her mind off this one.

The PD's lab had still been working on the body by the time the task force meeting wrapped up. Mike had told her they'd had to cut off the top of the freezer with a Sawzall in order to get Chelsea out.

There was something so disturbing about this killer. Most serials went out of their way to avoid attention, Emily knew. This one seemed to relish it. It was as if he wanted to rub their noses in what he was doing.

What had he said? *"Tell Mom I said hi."* Even for a sociopath predator, the callousness and arrogance of it was mind-blowing. This guy wasn't just confident, he was cocky. With the exception of letting the one drug dealer spot him, he hadn't made a single mistake.

Twenty laps later, Emily Parker carded back into her room and called home.

"How is she?" she asked her brother, Tom.

"You're going to love this, Em. Today, one of Olivia's knucklehead boy classmates overheard the teacher call her Olivia Jacqueline and then proceeded to call her OJ Parker for the rest of the morning."

"That little bum," Emily said.

"No, wait," her brother said, laughing. "The kid's name is Brian Kevin Sullivan, so the Olive dubbed him BK Sullivan. Now everybody calls him Burger King Sullivan. How do you like that? I think Burger King is going to think twice next time he wants to mess with the Olive."

Emily couldn't help but chuckle.

"Where is she now?"

"She's in bed. Her My Twinn doll came for a sleepover tonight, so quarters are a little tight. She wanted to remind you that the American Girl store is on Fifth Avenue. And to make sure you say hi to Eloise at the Plaza Hotel."

"Done," Emily said, feeling a lightness in her heart that was sorely needed. "You're the best uncle who ever lived, Tom."

"Don't forget the best brother," he said. "Stay safe."

As she hung up, she noticed that someone had left a message. Listening, she heard Mike's voice, and she called him back.

"What now?" she said when he picked up.

"Nothing," Bennett said. "I just wanted to let you know that there haven't been any kidnappings in the past half hour."

She thought of him. Their lunch, the wonderful dinner with his family. She sat staring at the utter loneliness of her room, her life. She hadn't even thought of getting involved with anyone since her husband had abandoned ship. The more time she spent with Mike, though, the more she was starting to consider the possibility.

"Where are you now, Mike?" she discovered herself saying.

What the hell was she doing!

"I can't hear you. One of these kids is screaming bloody murder. Hang on. There. I'm in the kitchen now. What did you say?"

Emily thought about it. She had to stop. A cop? In another city? How the hell would that work?

"Nothing," she said. "See you in the morning, Mike."

Chapter 34

I STOOD THERE in my kitchen, staring at my cell phone.

There had been a moment there between us, some kind of hovering opportunity, but goddammit, I'd missed it somehow.

Still, it was nice just hearing her voice. Not as nice as seeing her face, but almost. She was a good cop, good for a laugh, and good-looking. All good, in my book. I felt like we'd known each other for two years instead of three days.

My phone rang while I was still standing there, pining like one of my love-struck tweens. Back to reality, Casanova, I thought.

It was my boss, Carol Fleming.

"Mike, I just heard some City Hall flack came by the task force for a copy of all your reports. You have any idea what the deputy mayor would want with them?"

"Unfortunately," I said, "we banged heads with Hottinger when the Dunning kid was snatched. She's probably just trying to make trouble for me, boss. Looking for something to jam me up."

"That anorexic bitch can pound sand," my boss said angrily. "Internal police records are strictly confidential, and if she wants information, it'll come from me personally. This case couldn't be run more professionally. Don't you worry about her or anyone else as long as I'm around. Get some sleep, Bennett."

Wow, I thought after I hung up. A boss who had confidence in me and who was willing to stick her neck out to protect me. That was a nice switch.

But about that sleep, I thought, walking out of the kitchen and staring at the wreckage that used to be my dining room table.

There were beakers, plastic tubing, stopwatches, food dye. Enough poster board to build a light aircraft.

Yep, it was that dreaded time of year again. Holy Name's annual science fair.

Six of my ten kids were furiously finishing their

projects. Jane was testing the soil in Riverside Park. Eddie was investigating the geometry of shadows. Brian was doing something on television watching and brainpower. Or was he just watching television instead of getting his work done? I wasn't exactly sure.

Even my five-year-old, Chrissy, had been enslaved by the science police. They had her making a stethoscope out of toilet tissue tubes. The Manhattan Project had taken less work.

I reached out as a streak of tinfoil went past my head.

"Is this ball yours, Trent?" I said, handing it back to him.

"That's not a ball, Dad," I was informed with a groan. "That's Jupiter."

After I'd gotten in from work, I'd been immediately dispatched to our local Staples for some last-minute items. I hadn't seen that many crazed-looking adults since April 15 at the post office. Didn't the guidelines say that the students were to put together their own experiments? Yeah, right.

Ten minutes before midnight, I tucked in the last of the Edisons and Galileos and headed for the kitchen.

With glue-speckled cheeks and Sharpie-stained

fingers, Mary Catherine was busy putting on all the finishing touches.

"Hey, Mary. I bet you never thought you'd have the pleasure of immersing yourself this deeply in the joys of science. Is your mind feeling as expanded as mine?"

"I have an idea for an experiment I'd like to run by those science people," she said as she twirled a pipe cleaner.

"How much stress can people take before their heads actually explode?"

Chapter 35

IT WAS 2:20 in the morning when Dan Hastings exited Butler, Columbia University's main library. Instead of heading toward the handicap ramp, the handsome blond freshman economics major smiled mischievously, zipped his iBOT wheelchair into stair mode, and rode the sucker all the way down the massive building's Greek temple stairs.

You'd think I'd have learned my lesson, he thought as the expensive computer-balanced wheelchair bounced hard off the last step. His legs had become paralyzed in a mountain-biking accident.

He'd been on an extreme adventure trip to the Orkhon Valley in Central Mongolia with his dad. One second he was flying down a jeep track like the reincarnated Genghis Khan, and the next, his front tire got jacked between a couple of boulders.

His landing at the bottom of the ravine had pulverized his ninth, tenth, and eleventh thoracic vertebrae, but he wasn't complaining. He still had his brain and his heart and, as a Mongolian parting bonus, the full use of his penis. With his iBOT, the so-called Ferrari of wheelchairs, he was putting the whole thing where it belonged. Behind him. He could and would continue to go anywhere he wanted.

Tonight's late studying marathon was due to a mother of a stats test he had the next day. That, and the fact that his roomie was hosting a party for his Peace Studies group. He'd rather sleep in the stacks than hang with those tree huggers.

If truth be known, he was the biggest conservative he'd ever met. At liberal Columbia, that made him a spy, embedded deep in enemy territory.

His chair's motor hummed as he opened it up across College Walk into Low Plaza. Usually, the area was filled with sunbathers and Hacky Sackers, but it was completely deserted now, the lit-up majestic dome of Low Library looking strangely ominous against the dark night sky.

Hadn't the antiwar hippies taken over that beautiful building during the sixties? What a disgrace.

What was even worse was that a lot of his fellow students still believed in that garbage.

Not him. He was an economics major. His original plan was to work his ass off, graduate summa, and get his ticket punched as an intern for one of the major Wall Street investment banks. But ever since Bear Stearns, Goldman, and Merrill had blown themselves up, he'd been thinking about trying to get on with a private-equity firm. He didn't care which, just so long as it was big.

Go big or go home in a Med-Lift chopper was pretty much the Dan Hastings credo.

He popped in his iPod earbuds and scrolled himself up a little Fall Out Boy. That and My Chemical Romance were the greatest in wheelchair-cruising tunes.

He was passing Lewisohn Hall when he saw the light. A strange blue strobing coming from a doorway on its south side. Was it a cell phone? He slowed the chair and tugged out his earbuds.

"Hey, Dan. C'mere," called a voice in a loud whisper.

What was up? Dan thought, zooming over. Was it somebody from one of his classes? College high jinks? Maybe it was a pantie raid. He was down with that. What was a pantie raid, anyway?

When he was about five feet away, Dan almost jerked out of his chair as he braked to a dead stop. A guy in a black pea coat and a ski mask stepped out of the doorway, holding a pistol.

What the fuck was this? And where the hell was Security?

He'd heard that Morningside Heights, the neighborhood around the Ivy League school, was notoriously dangerous, but he'd never heard of someone actually being mugged on campus.

"Take it," Dan said, offering him the iPod. "There's a hundred and fifty dollars and an American Express card in the wallet in my bag. You can have that, too, buddy."

"Gee, aren't you nice?" the man wearing the ski mask said as he grabbed Dan by his jacket and ripped him full out of the chair. The service door beside the man boomed as he kicked it open.

"What the fuck are you doing?" Dan cried as he was carried into the dark building.

The man hoisted him over his knee and violently wrapped his arms, legs, and mouth with masking tape.

"Shhh," the man said, slinging him over his shoulder. "Quiet down now. No talking in class."

Part Three

SIGN OF THE CROSS

Chapter 36

"DAD, DON'T TRIP, and whatever you do, please don't drop it!" Jane called after me as I zombie-shuffled over the curb toward Holy Name's auditorium, bearing the awkward display boards.

Though the science projects were officially completed, this next stage was like on the Food Network show where the contestants have to move their cakes to the judging table.

Only I had to do it six times, and there would be no chance for a $10,000 check.

Once everything had been safely transported, I started to relax, though when I passed a blood pressure cuff on one of the gymnasium's many displays, I was tempted to test mine.

I walked Chrissy to her kindergarten class's door. She pulled away from me as I went to give her a hug.

"Not here, Daddy. They'll say I'm a baby," she told me.

But you are a baby, I thought.

"Can't we at least shake hands, Miss Bennett?" I said. She gave me a quick, businesslike pump and bolted off without looking back. I smiled from the door as she linked arms and began whispering in earnest with one of her classmates. The kids were all growing up so quickly.

Thank God I, miraculously, wasn't aging with them.

I was coming down the school's front steps when I noticed that I hadn't turned on my phone after charging it. No wonder my morning had been filled with peace and quiet.

Uh-oh, I thought. In the past twenty minutes, there had been two messages from my boss and four from Emily Parker. I called Emily back first. She was cuter.

"What now?" I said.

"The Fox Channel. Turn it on."

I ducked into Holy Name's rectory, adjoining the school. Mrs. Maynard, the parish secretary, looked up from stuffing envelopes at her desk.

"Father Bennett is still saying the eight o'clock, Mike," she said to me.

"Is he? Could I borrow your TV?" I said, going into the lounge beside her without waiting for an answer.

"Live Breaking News," said the text in the corner of the local Fox Channel's screen. Across the bottom I read, MEDIA BARON'S SON MISSING. There was a shaky aerial shot of a college campus, probably taken from a helicopter. I recognized the granite dome of Columbia's Low Memorial Library. Police were laying tape by another campus building while a growing crowd watched.

"No," I said into my phone as I finally made out what the police were cordoning off. The camera had zoomed in on an empty wheelchair.

I felt like borrowing the rosary beads around the crucifix on the wall beside the TV. He'd taken another kid? This horror was nonstop. Was that the point? Damn it, this was all we needed!

"Where are you now, Emily?" I said as I hit the street.

"Running to the subway. Columbia's uptown, right?" she said. "Don't bother picking me up. I'll meet you there."

Chapter 37

"WHERE TO, MIKE?" Mary Catherine said as I hopped back into our van. "Starbucks? That diner on Eleventh? No, how about we score a couple of warm H and H bagels and eat them in the park? I'm famished after that all-nighter."

"Change of plans, Mary Catherine," I said. "Another kid just got kidnapped. I have to head over to Columbia yesterday."

Mary Catherine's eyes lit up as she revved the engine. She was a notorious lead foot.

"Hit the lights, Starsky. I'll get you there in no time."

On our way to Columbia, I called Chief Fleming.

"There you are," she said. "The press found out about it before we did. Are you there yet?"

"Just about."

"The TV is saying that it's the media mogul Gordon Hastings's son, but that hasn't been confirmed."

"That'll be the first thing on my list," I said as we arrived at the campus.

A mob of students and press had crowded into Low Plaza, at 116th and Broadway. Sirens split the air every few seconds as more and more police cars arrived.

I saw Emily Parker emerge from the subway and called to her.

"Oh, I see," Mary Catherine said, glaring at her through the windshield. "You didn't say *she* was going to be here."

"Of course," I said as I got out. "She's a kidnapping expert with the FBI. This looks like a kidnapping. What is it, Mary?"

"Oh, nothing. It's none of my business what you do, Mike," she said as she revved the van and ripped the transmission into gear.

"Or who you do it with. You're welcome for the ride," she said as she peeled off.

She whipped a screeching U-ee. I stood gaping as she dropped the hammer down Broadway.

Had she gone completely over the edge? Must have been the science fair, I thought.

"Was that your nanny?" Emily said as she arrived at a jog beside me.

"I'm not really sure," I said.

Chapter 38

FRANCIS X. MOONEY carried a briefcase and a venti latte as he hurried with the morning rush-hour crowd through Grand Central Terminal. He was approaching the famous clock at the station's center when he spotted the girl at the end of one of the Metro North ticket lines. He halted, weak suddenly, his heart snaring, unable to breathe.

The milky skin, the long black hair. *My God, it was her!* he thought, panicking. He'd messed up somehow! Chelsea Skinner was right there. She was still alive!

When the young woman turned to open her purse, the spell was broken. Francis felt a head rush of relief as he realized it was actually a thirty-something businesswoman, much too tall and heavy to be the young woman he had abducted and shot.

What the hell was wrong with him? he thought as he unrooted himself. Things were getting to him. The lack of sleep, the physical exertion. He was losing it, actually hallucinating.

He stopped at a line of Verizon phone kiosks. He removed the vial of Ritalin that sat beside the 9-millimeter Browning at the bottom of his briefcase.

He'd been practically living on amphetamines for the past three weeks, Adderall, meth, bennies. He'd read somewhere that the air force gave its pilots amphetamines to keep them alert on long-range missions.

He was on a mission, too, wasn't he? The most important mission the world had ever known. He needed anything and everything that could keep him going.

After he swallowed half a dozen pills, he took off his glasses and laid his forehead against the aluminum coin slot. The thunder of feet on the station's marble seemed to triple in volume as the speed cut into his bloodstream. He put his glasses back on and made a laser line for the bustling station's Lexington Avenue exit.

Directly across Lex, he entered the marble-and-stainless-steel lobby of the Chrysler Building. He shifted the latte to his case hand as he passed his company's electronic pass over the security turnstile's scanner.

His law firm's shining brass ERICSSON, WEYMOUTH AND ROTH sign greeted him outside the elevator on the sixty-first floor. At twenty-nine, he'd been the youngest to ever make partner. There was a time he'd wanted, and probably could have gotten, the name Mooney added to that sign.

That time was long over. In fact, this was his very last day.

He made a quick left before the glass door that led to his firm's reception desk and snuck in through the back way. He needed to keep a low profile. Calling in sick the whole week before, he'd caused a caseload logjam of startling proportions. At his *Forbes* 100, top-flight, bill-or-die corporate firm, erratic attendance was a sin equivalent to pissing on the senior partner's desk.

His personal assistant, Carrie, almost fell out of her chair as he ducked into her cubicle.

"Francis! What a happy surprise. I wasn't sure if you'd be able to make it in. I was just about to call you. Your nine o'clock, Steinman, just called. Something came up at the studio, he said. He won't be in New York until next Thursday."

Francis breathed down a spike of anger. "Something came up at the studio" was Hollywood bullshit for "the check is in the mail." He'd only decided to waste time and risk coming in because of the potential good that could have come out of the meeting with the multimillionaire movie executive.

He'd been stupid. He was trying to accomplish everything, but even flying on speed that was impossible.

"And, oh," Carrie said, lifting a memo sheet out of her in-box, "I heard from reception that Kurt from New York Heart called last Friday. He said it was urgent."

New York Heart was a privately funded antipoverty organization that Mooney did pro bono work for. He'd been advising them on a case about a destitute Harlem man who was on death row in Florida.

Francis winced. With everything else going on, he'd forgotten all about it. An urgent message about a death-row appeal couldn't be good.

He thought about his plans. His time frame. It would be an incredible crunch, but he had to try. Even with everything he'd put into motion, he didn't have a choice but to swing by the charity.

"Drop everything and cancel the rest of my meetings

until further notice, would you, Carrie? I have to head up there."

"Are you sure you should, Francis?" Carrie whispered with concern. "You haven't been here for a week. I think some of the clients, and even more so the junior partners, have been complaining, Mr. M. In fact, Mr. Weymouth is livid. Is there anything I can do? Do you need someone to talk to?"

Francis smiled at his personal assistant's concern. Ever since she'd begun working for him seven years before, she'd been terrific, so smart and precise and loyal.

When it all came out, would she understand what he had tried to do? Would anyone?

That was beside the point, he thought, steeling himself. It didn't matter what people thought about him personally. It wasn't about him.

He planted a kiss on her forehead.

"You're sweet to think about me, Carrie, but believe it or not, I've never felt better in all my life," he said as he headed back for the elevators.

Chapter 39

THERE WAS AN unimpeded view of the empty wheelchair from the window of Columbia's Department of Public Safety. Standing at the window, staring at the chair, Jesse Acevedo, the Campus Security chief, seemed incapable of doing anything except shaking his head.

"That's going to be the cover of the *Post,*" he said, more to himself than to anyone else. "I mean, that's my job, right? A handicapped student gets snatched on campus? Oh, I'm sorry, the handicapped son of one of the world's most powerful men. My daughter goes here. Once I'm out, no more staff scholarship. What the hell am I going to do?"

I felt bad for the guy. I knew full well the kind of

bullshit blame he'd be getting. But I didn't have the time to sympathize.

"Tell us about the tunnels again," I said.

"Shit, I'm sorry," he said, coming back to his desk. When his phone rang, he lifted the receiver and clicked it back in its cradle. When it rang again, he unclipped the phone cord from the back of it.

"The tunnels," he said after a deep breath. "Right. The tunnels connect some of the campus buildings. Lewisohn, the one next to where we found the empty chair, has tunnels that go to Havemeyer, Math, and the Miller Theater. There's another, older one that actually goes under Broadway to one of the Barnard College buildings on the other side of Broadway."

"Reid Hall. I know," I said.

We'd already found that the basement door in that building had been propped open. John Cleary and his CSU team were there now, going over every square inch of the basement with an evidence vacuum and Q-tips. The killer must have gotten in and taken the kid out through there.

"Who else knows about the tunnels?" Emily said.

"Students, maintenance, faculty," he said. "We blocked off some of them, but the kids still use them as shortcuts sometimes. Like hotels, every campus has its ghost stories, and the tunnels figure in a lot of the urban legends that get told around here."

I kept thinking about the kidnapper's cultured, educated voice. He most definitely could have been an Ivy League academic.

"One more question," I said. "Has a teacher ever been caught down there?"

"I don't know," Acevedo said. "I'll look into it and let you know. Or at least I'll leave a note for my replacement."

"I'm actually starting to respect this nut," Emily said as we headed down the stairs. "I've never seen someone so prolific. This guy is a gold-medal-winning kidnapper."

Emily ducked into the cafeteria on the ground floor of the building and came back with two coffees. This morning, she was wearing a form-fitting French Blue blouse and navy skirt. Her hair was still wet. I liked that she wore hardly any makeup. The way she did a cute earlobe-tugging thing when she was thinking, and especially the spark that flashed in her blue eyes when she was fired up.

"Now what?" Emily said. "Head over to Hastings's dorm? The library where he was last seen?"

"Nah," I said. "We better head to the family. I'm expecting a call from our friend."

Chapter 40

THE HARLEM SATELLITE office of the social service, nonprofit New York Heart was on 134th Street off St. Nicholas Avenue. The sour scent of sweat and marijuana made Francis X. Mooney nostalgic as he mounted the unswept stairs two by two.

For the past ten years, Mooney had been the main adviser of their legal outreach program, which took on cases for the poorest of the poor. He stared at the posters and photographs of the organization's community theater and community garden that covered the stairwell walls and smiled. New York Heart was truly a labor of love.

"What's cooking, kids?" Francis said after he

gathered the half dozen social workers in the cramped conference room ten minutes later.

Francis X. smiled around the battered table at the lanky twenty-somethings. He remembered being that young, having that fire in the belly to set things straight. Not every young person was a selfish, whining brat, he thought.

"I just got your message this morning, Kurt," he said. "How's Mr. Franklin's case going?"

Kurt, the social service's in-house law advocate, looked up from his bagel and cream cheese. He'd gone to Fordham and hadn't passed the bar yet, but Francis had faith in him. The kid's heart was in the right place.

"The reason I called is that Mr. Franklin's last appeal pretty much got slam-dunked into the shitter, Francis," he said between bites. "The fuckers are going to fry him this Friday, and the rednecks down there will probably tailgate in the prison parking lot. What are you going to do? Hope the Republicans are happy. Another one bites the dust."

Francis couldn't believe it as chuckles exploded around the room. Mr. Reginald Franklin, the son of a destitute local resident, and borderline retarded, was about to be executed by the American government. How was that funny?

"Did you look over the habeas corpus?" Francis said.

"Of course," Kurt said. "The appeals court decided to go by the trial record."

"That's what they always do," Francis said, raising his voice now. "Did you get a copy of the police report, like I told you to? Did you look into the adequacy of his first attorney? The man supposedly fell asleep at one point."

The room was silent now. Kurt set his bagel on the table as he sat up.

"No, I didn't get a chance," he finally said. "I did call you."

"Didn't get a chance? Didn't get a chance!" Francis yelled. His chair made a thunderous shriek as he leapt up. "Are you out of your fucking mind? The man is about to die!"

"Jeez, Francis," Kurt mumbled with his head down. "Relax."

"I won't," Francis X. said. He didn't want to cry. Not in front of these kids, but he couldn't help it. A torrent of hot tears poured down his reddened face.

"I can't relax, don't you see?" he said as he stormed out. "There's no more time."

Chapter 41

WE WERE OUT on Columbia's sprawling Low Plaza, heading over to the bursar's office to get Dan Hastings's personal info, when my phone rang.

"Mike," Detective Schultz cried. "Get over quick to the vice president's office at the Low Memorial Library. We need your help. You're not going to believe this."

I met a frustrated-looking Schultz and Ramirez in a hallway on the second floor of the college's iconic domed building. The administration was denying them the tapes from the Campus Security cameras due to "privacy concerns."

"These wackos are acting like we're the KGB rounding up people for the gulag instead of trying to save the life of one of their kidnapped students," Ramirez said wide-eyed.

After twenty minutes of arguing, it finally took the threat of both a city and federal subpoena to get the officials to release the tapes, along with Dan Hastings's personal information.

"Only in New York," Agent Parker said as we went out toward the Broadway gate and the Crown Victoria that the FBI's New York office had dropped off for her.

"Or any Ivy League college campus," I said.

The victim's father, Gordon Hastings, lived way downtown on Prince Street in SoHo. As Emily drove, I listened to a 1010 WINS report that was already being broadcast about him. Gordon Hastings used to work for Rupert Murdoch and now had his own business buying radio and TV stations, mostly in Canada and Europe. His wealth was estimated at eight hundred million dollars. I couldn't even imagine that kind of money. Or what the man had to be going through, knowing that his disabled son had been abducted.

As she drove, Emily called the New York office and ran Gordon Hastings through NCIC and other federal databases.

"He was born and raised in Scotland," she said, hanging up a few minutes later, "but became a U.S.

citizen a couple of years ago. He's clean, though the IRS has an open case on him due to some remarks he made about offshore accounts in a *Vanity Fair* interview."

"Imagine that," I said. "And all my *Vanity Fair* interviews always go so swimmingly."

I let out an angry snort a moment later as we turned off Broadway onto Prince.

Half a dozen news vans had beat us to Hastings's cast-iron building. Cold-eyed camera lenses swung on us as we double-parked. I swung my cold-eyed Irish face right back at them.

"No goddamn comment," I yelled at them as I got out. "And get that goddamn eyewitness van away from that fire hydrant if you ever want to see it again."

"Now, that's what I call media savvy," Emily said with a grin as we waded through the newsies on the sidewalk. "If you ever make it down to DC, you should toss your résumé into the ring for White House press secretary."

"You thought that was bad," I said. "I was being restrained. I usually just empty a magazine into the air."

It actually turned out that the ride we had taken downtown was for nothing. The luxury building's handsome but seemingly stoned concierge stifled a giggle when we asked to speak to Gordon Hastings.

"C'mon. Where you been, man? I thought everyone knew that only Mr. Hastings's second wife and new baby twins get to live in the penthouse duplex during the divorce proceedings."

"Could we speak to the soon-to-be ex–Mrs. Gordon Hastings, then?" Emily said before I could ask the guy for a urine sample.

"I wouldn't think so," the spaced-out model lookalike said. "Unless, of course, you're planning a trip to Morocco, where her Italian *Vogue* shoot is."

The only useful thing we learned was that the mogul's mail was being forwarded to somewhere called Pier Fifty-nine, at Twenty-third Street and the Hudson River.

It turned out to be the Chelsea Piers Sports Center. We stared at the kids Rollerblading and the men with golf bags on the sidewalk in front of it.

"That kid was even higher than he looked. How could this guy live at a sports facility?" Emily said as we pulled up.

"That's how," I said as I pointed to the yacht-filled marina beside the netted driving range.

Chapter 42

OVER TWO HUNDRED feet long, Gordon Hastings's yacht, the *Teacup Tempest,* turned out to be the largest one at the marina. Ten minutes later, we sat waiting to meet the mogul at the rear of its massive cherry-paneled forward salon.

There were antiques and paintings. There were also row upon row of flat-screen TVs. Smaller computer screens on scattered desks showed investment graphs. In addition to the ship's crew, there were eight or nine businesspeople, Hastings's corporate team that actually worked from the ship. Like us, they were just standing around waiting, with stressed-out looks on their faces.

The captain of the vessel, John McKnight, who'd

escorted us on board, told us about the accident that had crippled the abducted Columbia freshman.

"It was on a mountain-biking trip in Asia that was all Mr. H's idea," the captain said in a low voice. "He completely blames himself. That's what led to his divorce, if you want my opinion. Now with Dan being abducted, it's just unbelievable. Unbearable. For all of us. Dan was the most down-to-earth, lovable kid you ever met. He took the accident like it was nothing. He was inspiring."

"He still is inspiring as far as we know, Captain," I said. "You can't forget that."

A barefoot figure in a Hawaiian shirt and khakis finally emerged from one of the rear staterooms. The wiry, deeply tanned man came directly over to us and shook our hands, and we introduced ourselves. I noticed that his heavy gold watch had nautical flags on it instead of numbers. I could also see the top of his pajama pants above the waistband of his khakis. He didn't stagger or smell of alcohol, but I could tell the distraught father had been drinking.

"Thank you so much for coming," he said with an unexpected thick Scottish burr. With his bald head and mustache, he actually looked a little like Sean Connery. "Have you learned anything?"

"There's been nothing so far, sir," Emily said. "I can't imagine what you must be going through."

He stared at Emily a moment and then a vicious look crossed his face.

"Maybe that lack of imagination is the reason why the first two victims ended up dead, Agent Parker," he said with a sneer. "I just bought the *New York Mirror* a few weeks ago, you know. One hears these things."

Wow, I thought. Looks like James Bond, acts like Attila the Hun. And make that drinking *heavily*. I understood that Hastings was hurting, but his nastiness was inappropriate and completely uncalled for.

"The pattern of the man who kidnapped Jacob Dunning and Chelsea Skinner is to contact the family," I said, edging myself between Emily and Hastings. "We don't know if the person or persons who seem to have taken your son are the same, but we'll go on that assumption. With your permission, we'd like to put trap-and-trace equipment on your phones."

"I guess . . . ," Hastings said, brooding.

"Thank you, sir," Emily continued with a grin. "You wouldn't happen to know either the Dunnings or the Skinners by any chance, would you?"

"Of course not," Hastings spat at her again. "What

kind of question is that? Do you think we're part of some billionaire cabal? Don't they have any actual professionals who take care of kidnappings?"

"Right here, sir," Emily said with an even wider, lovelier smile. "You're looking at them. Thank you again for your cooperation."

"Way to handle that jackass, Parker," I said as the millionaire left.

"I've learned from the best, Mike," Emily said, grinning.

Chapter 43

OUTSIDE, EMILY AND I huddled with our own team and got busy bringing in the phone-tracing gear from the FBI and NYPD tech cars in the marina's lot. In addition to recording the conversation, the tech guys were going to run it through voice-analysis software, a kind of high-tech lie detector and emotion indicator. We hooked up my phone to the equipment as well this time.

We'd just finished setting everything up when something sounded from one of the computers in the luxury salon's corner.

"You've got mail," it said in an inappropriately cheery tone.

"I didn't know they actually still said that," I said to Hastings's secretary.

"They really don't, but Mr. Hastings insists. He finds it nostalgic," she said in a way that implied it was one of many nutty insistences that came from Emperor Hastings.

We rushed over. Mr. Hastings's personal assistant quickly brought up the mail page.

From	Subject
danhastings@AOL.com	Whether I live or die

The secretary bit her lip as she opened the e-mail.

> Hastings,
> If you want to see your son alive again, you'll get five million dollars in hundred-dollar denominations ready for delivery. You have three hours. The faster we wrap this up, the faster you can get back to your greedy, decadent life.
>
> I do not think I need to remind you what I am capable of.

"What is it?" Hastings said, emerging from his stateroom. He banged a shin on a settee as he rushed over and stared at the screen. Everyone jumped as he emitted a primal moan.

"Oh, Danny! Oh, my son," Hastings said. He knocked a lamp off the desk as he reached for the computer monitor. Luckily, he missed. He landed with a painful-sounding thump next to the lamp on the Oriental rug.

We watched as Captain McKnight lifted Hastings from the floor. It looked like something he'd done before. He spoke to him soothingly as he guided him to the back of the ship.

Vivid freeze-frame images of Jacob Dunning and Chelsea Skinner flashed through my head as I reread the last part of the e-mail.

I do not think I need to remind you what I am capable of.

No, he didn't, I thought. He was right about that.

Chapter 44

AS OUR TECHS got busy tracing the e-mail, I caught Emily's attention.

"Could I talk to you out on the aloha deck?" I said, motioning for the salon's exit.

On our way outside, through an open doorway I spotted a dining room set with crystal and silver for twenty. I found the sight of it, for some reason, the most lonesome thing.

No wonder Hastings had gone over the edge. Even with eight hundred million dollars, life had rammed him completely through the wringer. Despite his drunken melodrama, I truly felt sorry for him.

"I don't like this, Parker," I said as we stood outside, watching yuppies hit golf balls on the converted dock beside us. "Something smells. On the one hand, switching to e-mail is in keeping with our guy's pattern of changing methods. But on the other hand, our guy loves the sound of his voice too much to send an e-mail. He loves talking to me, crying on my shoulder. I'm not convinced this is the same guy."

Ramirez suddenly stuck his head outside.

"Mike, get in here quick. And I thought Columbia was bad. Now this is really getting nuts."

Back inside, I saw a large, bald gentleman in a pinstripe suit collecting the laptops off the desks.

"Sic 'em, Vin," Hastings yelled from a couch with a laugh. He lit a cigar. "Tell them their services are no longer required."

"Vinny Carbone," the new arrival said, offering his hand. "I'm Mr. Hastings's attorney. I'm going to be representing Mr. Hastings in this matter here."

I stared at Parker, baffled.

"I wasn't aware this was a court proceeding," I said.

"The bottom line is, you don't need to be putting any kind of trace software or spyware or anything else on Mr. Hastings's computers," the lawyer continued. "He's had a little trouble with you guys, especially the IRS, and, well, we're sorry, but we can't cooperate. In fact, you can get off his phones, too. He wants to handle things on his own from here. And if you've left any bugs, you should take them with you. We will be sweeping the whole boat after you leave."

Spyware and bugs? I thought. These people really were worse than the nuts at Columbia.

"Mr. Carbone," I said, putting up my palms. "This is a kidnapping. Dan Hastings is a citizen. We can't just walk away."

"Tell him to get the fuck off my boat, Vinny," the father yelled, pointing his stogie for emphasis. "Tell him we'll do it the right way. By ourselves. I let these assholes handle it, Dan comes back in a plastic bag."

"You heard it from the horse's mouth, kid," the lawyer said in his Brooklyn accent. "You gotta go."

More like the other end of the horse, I thought.

"Yeah, in a second, Pop," I said to Carbone, stepping past him.

"This might not even be the same kidnapper," I said to the father, trying not to lose my cool.

Emily, following me, seemed to have lost hers.

"You think you can buy your kid back?" she said loudly. "You're going to get him killed."

"Piss off, cop," Hastings said. "You're oh for two! You fools have no idea what you're doing."

He waved his cigar at us dismissively. He suddenly

sounded a lot less upper crust than at our initial meeting.

“Oh, don’t worry. I am pissed off, Mr. Hastings,” Emily yelled at him as we left. “I’ve been pissed off pretty much since the second I met you.”

Chapter 45

VINNY CARBONE, ESQUIRE, followed Emily and me back outside to the observation deck.

"Are you as insane as that guy? This is a federal investigation," Parker said to the lawyer.

"Hold on a second, Agent Parker," I said, pulling her back. "I think I can work this out.

"Listen, Vinny. You want subpoenas, you got 'em. But I guarantee you, I'll be going over his computers and phone records with a fine-tooth comb now. I'll lock his ass up for obstruction of justice—or shit, maybe I'll make him my main suspect. You gonna muzzle him, or do I take his rich drunken ass up to Harlem for questioning?"

Vin didn't think about my offer for too long. For

all his blue-collar demeanor, he definitely seemed on the ball.

"I'll talk to him," Vin said. "Gimme a sec."

As we waited, Parker and I stared at the cars on the West Side Highway, trying to brainstorm.

"We need to piece this thing together before this idiot really does get his son killed," Emily said.

"Okay, Parker," I said. "For the moment, let's assume it's the same guy. How does Dan Hastings fit in?"

"He's rich, obviously," Parker said. "One of the other two was a college freshman, too. He's an only child."

"No, he isn't," I pointed out. "He has two new half siblings, remember?"

"You're right," she said. "Is that important?"

"I don't know. It's a difference. Also, this guy's going through a divorce. The other two families were happily married."

"Good point. But doesn't that indicate another kidnapper?"

"Or that there's another connection we haven't made."

"Yeah, well, we better make it quick," Parker said as we watched an armored car pull into the pier's parking lot.

Two armed uniformed guards got out of the car, went around to the back, and removed two very large currency bags.

"Because this ship of fools looks like it's about to set sail."

Chapter 46

WE WERE ALLOWED back on board with the stipulation that our technicians be closely monitored by Gordon Hastings's staff. Hastings's IT adviser actually stood over the shoulder of our FBI techie as he installed a Computer and Internet Protocol Address Verifier.

The petty squabbling was still going on when the next "You've got mail" came at three o'clock on the button. Hastings himself opened up the e-mail.

> The following instructions will be followed to the letter.
>
> 1. The five million dollars will be placed in a black rolling suitcase.

2. You and you alone will bring the money to the south playground of the Polo Grounds projects at 155th Street in Harlem at 4:45 PM.
3. When you are there and when we are convinced you have not been followed or brought the police, you will be given more instructions.

Take note:

If there is any evidence of ground or air police surveillance, you will never see your son again.

The first two were to prove what I am capable of. You alone have been given the chance to save your precious flesh and blood. Do not blow it.

Hastings and his lawyer disappeared into the stateroom for a quick powwow. Carbone emerged five minutes later alone.

"Mr. Hastings will be paying the money and delivering it himself. That's nonnegotiable. He'll wear a wire so he can be kept track of, but that's it. Otherwise, follow the kidnapper's instructions. No air surveillance. Hear me, Bennett?"

I knew at some point in this case I'd be required

to apply the skills I'd learned as a hostage negotiator. I just never thought I'd have to use them in dealing with the victim's father.

We reluctantly had to agree. It really was up to Hastings how he wanted to play things, especially with the ransom. But that didn't mean we would shirk our responsibility and not use everything within our power to get his son back alive.

Emily and I quickly made calls to our respective agencies to relate how badly things were stacking up. My boss, Carol Fleming, told me she'd heard of Hastings's mouthpiece, Carbone. The lawyer was known to represent mob types.

Could that fit into this? I didn't know. But we didn't really have the time to check it out. We had a deadline in less than two hours, and we needed our people in place yesterday.

Standing by the bar, Mr. Hastings was drinking coffee now as our techs wired him up. His corporate people were busy packing the money. I understood the instructions for it to be in a rolling suitcase, because even in hundred-dollar bills, the ransom would weigh almost ninety pounds.

"This guy can hardly tie his shoes. How's he going to save his son?" Emily said.

"He's not," I said. "We are."

Chapter 47

DETECTIVES RAMIREZ AND Schultz had to stay and rough it back at the yacht as Emily and I raced up the West Side Highway and then crosstown along 155th Street. Traffic wasn't so bad, but then again, we didn't bother stopping for any of the red lights.

Housing Police sergeant Jack Bloom from Police Service Area 4 met us at the rear of the Polo Grounds Housing Project's most southern building.

"We patrol up here with guns drawn," the Housing cop advised as we arrived on the roof. "There's sexual assaults, beatings. We beg Housing to keep the roof doors locked, but they keep saying they can't because of fire codes. Even when you're patrolling the courtyards below, you need one eye up in case some kid wants to send you a little airmail."

There was an incredible view of Yankee Stadium across the Harlem River. Bloom told us that the projects were built where the historic Polo Grounds baseball stadium had been located.

"Get out of here," Emily said. "You mean the Giants-win-the-pennant,shot-heard-round-the-world Polo Grounds?"

Bloom nodded grimly.

"The only shots heard round here anymore are from the drug disputes in the stairwells."

"Well, it's definitely another hellhole like the other two locations," I said to Emily. "So maybe it is our guy, after all."

Twenty minutes later, we were radioed that Gordon Hastings was present and accounted for, waiting with the money in a town car half a block west on 155th. I checked my watch. It was four thirty. Fifteen minutes to contact.

Everything that could be set up was ready to go. Though not actually in the air, Aviation was waiting in Highbridge Park a little farther uptown. A Harbor Unit boat was on standby as well a little ways south down the Harlem River, in case anything was thrown into the water.

Two ESU surveillance teams and a contingent of the FBI's Hostage Rescue Team were getting in place inside several apartments surrounding the development's south playground. Over the radio, I could hear them aligning frequencies with one another.

If our guy was dumb enough to show up, we would bag him. I truly hoped he was.

I let out a tight, tense breath as I stared down at the project yards. For the first time, we had something the kidnapper wanted. We had to bet our only chip very carefully now.

Five minutes later, Emily called me over to the roof wall.

"Mike, check it out."

Down on the plaza beside the playground, some young black men in traditional African garb were setting up instruments. A moment later, a rhythmic drumming filled the courtyard.

"Nice beat," I said. "You want to African dance?"

"No, idiot," Emily said. "That's us. They're from the New York office's Special Surveillance group."

"No way," I said, laughing.

Emily nodded.

"The guy in the green buba and gbarie pants is the SAC for the White Collar Squad. What time do you have?"

"T minus ten minutes," I said, wiping sweat off my face.

Chapter 48

THE WIND AND my heart rate both picked up as Hastings finally exited his car on Clayton Powell Jr. Boulevard. I tracked the harried-looking father through the stark cement courtyard with a pair of high-power Nikon binoculars.

"Be advised," crackled the voice of a member of one of the surveillance teams over the radio. "Male black in a brown leather jacket is approaching from the south."

Agent Parker and I scurried over to the southeast corner of the roof. Directly below our vantage point, a young, bald black man wearing sunglasses was moving through the southern parking lot, making a beeline for Hastings.

He called out as Hastings was entering the courtyard's amphitheater. I turned up the other radio, which was tuned to Hastings's body mic.

"Over here," the man was saying.

Hastings stopped. He stood, breathing loudly, both hands now clutching the suitcase as the man approached.

"Where is Danny?" he said. "Where's my son?"

Ignoring him, the man took an already opened cell phone out of his pocket and handed it to Hastings.

Even without the binoculars, I probably could have detected the happiness that flashed across the father's face a second later.

"Oh, Danny!" he said, beginning to cry. "It's you! My God, I thought you were dead. Are you all right? Are you in pain?"

I felt a short jolt of relief as I exchanged a surprised look with Emily. Our abductor had slaughtered his first two victims pretty much outright. The fact that Dan Hastings still seemed to be alive was a very welcome sudden change of MO.

"I'm going to get you back now, Danny," the mogul said. "I'm going to do what they say. You're going to make it back home to me. I—"

The mogul's joyful expression fled as suddenly as it had appeared. The kidnapper must have gotten on the line. It was extremely frustrating not being able to hear both sides of the conversation.

"Yes, of course I have the money," Hastings said. "But you won't get one penny until my son is released."

We watched helplessly as Hastings listened to something the kidnapper was saying.

"Look where? At the phone?" Hastings finally said.

The mogul lifted the phone off his ear and looked at its screen.

What was happening now? Was he being shown a picture? A live video feed?

"Does anyone have a view of the phone? What's he looking at?" I called into the surveillance radio.

"It's someone in a wheelchair maybe," one of the HRT snipers cut in. "I can barely make it out."

"Okay, okay, good," Hastings said finally. He pushed the money at the man with the phone.

Whatever Hastings had seen had obviously convinced him that they were releasing his son. I wasn't there yet.

"Take it now. It's all there. It's yours," Hastings said. "I've done what you said. Now let Danny go."

Chapter 49

THE BLACK MAN was kneeling, zipping open the case to check the money, when Emily and I broke into a sprint toward the roof door. We needed to get down to the street to follow the money now. It was the only thing that would lead us to Hastings's son.

"He's on the move to the south, heading toward Bradhurst," came a voice over the radio as we hit the courtyard two minutes later.

"I'll follow on foot," I called to Emily as I spotted the tall youth moving south across the project yard. "Follow in the car. Stay at least two blocks behind me. The trunk of the Fed car has more antennas than a goddamn cell site. We don't want to spook him."

Emily booked away as I tailed the man. I hung

back as far as I could. He wasn't moving particularly fast. He didn't look over his shoulder or seem concerned in any way about whether anyone was following him. I wondered if he was being coy or if he was just stupid. I was leaning toward the latter.

As I followed, I stayed in contact with the roving multilayered surveillance detail we had set up. The topography of that little corner of East Harlem was hell on surveillance. Not only did we have the river, the Harlem River Drive, and a close subway to contend with, but the projects themselves were separated from the rest of Harlem by a high, stone bluff. There were lots of alleys, one-way streets, and dead ends, plenty of places to duck into to try to shake us.

It was cat-and-mouse time, and frankly, I wasn't exactly sure who was going to come out on top.

I was surprised when the man made a hard right out of the complex and headed under the raised roadway of 155th Street past a ROAD CLOSED sign. I noticed some cars parked at the dead end of the short street. Would he hop into one of them?

Instead, he made another right at the face of the dead end's stone bluff and turned toward a set of ascending stairs I hadn't seen. I shook my head when I reached them and saw how incredibly steep they were.

I wasn't sure if it was my thighs or my lungs that were burning the most as I neared the top.

"We have a visual," I heard over my radio as the man hit the top of the stairs next to a Harlem River Drive entrance ramp. We had an undercover Highway Patrol unit stationed a hundred yards north up the highway in case he attempted to move the money out that way.

He didn't, though. He passed the entrance and was crossing over Edgecombe Avenue along the upper part of 155th Street when I got to the top. I thought he would head down into the subway on the corner of 155th and St. Nicholas, where yet another team was waiting, but he surprised us all by heading to the window of a place called Eagle Pizza on the corner and grabbing a slice.

A slice? I thought. Was this guy for real? Nobody could be this calm. I searched the crowd of pedestrians going up and down the subway stairs. There was definitely something off about this whole thing.

Emily pulled up beside me, and I joined her in the Fed car. We watched the black guy finish his slice and continue west with the money.

He'd just rolled the suitcase off the next corner when it happened. There was a high scream of a motor, and a figure wearing a black motorcycle helmet and matching racing leathers roared up on a BMX dirt bike.

Without stopping and without an opportunity to do anything except look on with our mouths open, we watched as the rider scooped up the bag the black guy had let go of. He gunned the cycle through the red light, almost hitting the hood of our car, and raced the opposite way down 155th.

Chapter 50

WE WERE POINTED in the wrong direction as he lasered past us. Emily hopped the curb as she U-turned after him. I was on the radio, screaming the recent happenings, when the biker screeched to the left north onto Amsterdam. The biker swung off the street onto the sidewalk and into a city park. It felt like the axle broke as Emily hopped curb number two directly after him.

"I guess this means we're not maintaining tailing distance anymore!" I yelled as we violently off-roaded on the uneven grass behind the dirt bike.

The rider skidded to a stop beside a city pool. He left the bike and began booking with the money into the trees. I didn't have time to say, "You've got to be shitting me," as I jumped out after him.

I made it through a break in the thick brush and gulped as I spotted where the guy was headed.

It was the High Bridge pedestrian bridge, which connected Manhattan to the Bronx. Built in the mid-1800s, the thirteen-story narrow stone walkway that spanned the Harlem River had originally been used as an aqueduct that carried the city's water supply down from upstate. Now it was an abandoned structure just south of the Cross Bronx Expressway that city administrations debated whether they should renovate or tear down.

Motorcycle man swung the bag onto his back, hopped onto some ancient scaffolding, and started climbing. In a moment, he hopped over a break in the razor wire and was hightailing it toward the Bronx over the bridge's weed-filled cobblestone pavers.

"Call the Bronx!" I radioed my backup. "The Forty-fourth Precinct. The crazy son of a bitch is headed over the High Bridge walkway toward the Bronx!"

"And so's this one," I mumbled to myself as I tucked the radio into my pocket and pulled myself onto the scaffolding.

I paused as I hopped down from the fence onto the

bridge itself. It was maybe ten feet across, with only flimsy, waist-high cast-iron railings between me and a horrifying fall to my death. Talk about vertigo.

Motorcycle man was going flat out at the other end of the bridge when he shrugged the bag off his back and chucked it. I thought it would hit the river, but I saw it land with a puff of dust on the Bronx side between the Major Deegan Expressway and the Metro North train tracks.

"He tossed it!" I called. "Get somebody across the river and down by the train tracks. The money is next to the Bronx-side tracks!"

When I looked up, I saw the motorcycle man running in a new direction. Directly at me!

He had his jacket off and was grasping something in his hand now. It had wires coming out of it. They seemed to go over his shoulder toward his back.

Bomb!? I thought, drawing my Glock. *What the—?*

"DOWN! NOW!" I yelled. The guy was a bad listener.

"ON YOUR KNEES!" I yelled.

He kept coming. The sight of him, silently running at me for no conceivable reason, was beyond surreal. I was about to squeeze off a shot, when he did it. The craziest thing of all.

Without pausing, he veered to my left, bounded up onto the low iron railing, and dove without a sound off the bridge.

I think my heart actually stopped. I ran to my left and looked down. The guy was plummeting toward the water when there was a strange bloom of color that at first I thought was an explosion. I thought he'd blown himself up, but then I saw the orange canopy of a parachute.

Son of a bitch! I thought. He hadn't committed suicide. He'd base-jumped off the bridge. I knew I should have shot him! I debated whether I still should as he sailed up the river.

"Get Harbor and Aviation up!" I screamed. "The son of a bitch just did a James Bond off the bridge. He parachuted off. I repeat. He just parachuted off the bridge!"

Chapter 51

I THOUGHT WE were going to flip ten minutes later as Parker whipped us off the Bronx-side highway onto a Metro North utility road. We were still skidding to a stop when I hopped out of the car and over the third rail to the weeds where I thought the bag had landed.

I searched through the weeds like a man possessed. I kicked past a Prestone can, a Happy Meal box, several tires. Where the hell was it! That's when I saw the black strap. I rushed over and pulled. Shit! It was weightless. The bag was empty.

I decided to take a seat in the dead grass beside it. There was a path behind me that led less than a hundred feet up to the highway. The kidnappers must have been waiting. They were long gone.

We'd blown it. We'd lost the money.

"Shit and double shit," Emily said, when I showed her the empty bag. She offered her hand and pulled me up. "Harbor got the jumper at least. Let's go."

I was still firing full bore on adrenaline when I hopped out of the Fed car and crashed down a bank of the Harlem River to the north. Harbor had pulled the base jumper out of the drink and was holding him near the southbound entrance for the Cross Bronx Expressway.

With the help of one of the Harbor guys, I sat the parachutist up from where he was lying wet and handcuffed on his belly. He was a young, pimple-faced white kid with a frosted faux-Hawk haircut.

"This is over. Where is Dan Hastings? Where is he?" I yelled.

"What? Danny who?" the kid said, his face scrunched in surprise. "Is he a new guy on the team? The Birdhouse Team?"

I squinted my eyes into slits.

"You have two seconds to tell me what you're talking about before you go swimming in handcuffs."

"Hey, man. I didn't do anything. I was paid to

jump the bridge by this guy Mark. He said he was from Birdhouse—you know, the Tony Hawk skateboard company? He said they needed some crazy-ass footage for one of their new movies. I know it wasn't exactly legal, but he gave me ten grand cash. He said some black guy would drop a bag on the corner of Amsterdam, and I would bike it to the bridge and do my thing. He gave me half up front. I swear to God that's the truth."

I stared at the dopey kid, furious.

"What did you think when I was pointing my gun at you? I was method acting?"

"Yes," the kid said emphatically. "I thought it was all part of the movie, man. So, you're basically telling me the cameras weren't rolling?"

Could anyone be this stupid? I decided this guy could.

"They still are," I said as a couple of Bronx uniforms arrived. "This next scene is where you get thrown in prison."

Back at the car, I said to Emily, "The idiot says he was hired to jump the bridge, and I actually believe him."

That was a definite low point in the investigation. We'd lost the money and the trail back to Hastings's son. We got taken to the cleaners. We'd blown everything.

We were comparing notes with the rest of the shell-shocked surveillance guys when the victim's father, Gordon Hastings, showed up in his town car.

"You cocked it up! You lost my money! You killed my son!" the red-faced Scot screamed as he came for me across the shoulder of the highway.

He's lucky he didn't make it through the half dozen cops and agents between us. At that point I was so frustrated, I would gladly have knocked his millionaire teeth out, father or no father.

Chapter 52

FIVE MINUTES LATER, Parker and I spun over to the Thirtieth Precinct, where the two suspects in the money chase had been taken.

After a lost coin flip in the precinct captain's office, I was given the onerous task of calling in the fiasco to One Police Plaza. Even the ordinarily heartless, map-of-Ireland-faced precinct captain O'Dwyer gave me a sympathetic nod before leaving me to my spanking. Having dropped the full payload of bad tidings, I thought my ears would start hemorrhaging from the chief's tongue-lashing.

I was still licking my wounds in one of the captain's Ed Koch–administration plastic chairs when

Emily came back in from the suspect interview rooms down the hall.

"Same story," she said, closing her notebook and collapsing into the traffic cone–orange chair next to me. "The bald black guy and the kid were both paid in cash by the mysterious Mark. They describe him as a very burly white biker type. They said he had a red Abraham Lincoln beard and double sleeves of tats. Another disguise, maybe?"

I shrugged.

"I can't believe it," I said. "After all that, we're back to square one. Make that square negative one."

Dan Hastings was gone. The five million dollars was gone. I'd come very close to killing a reckless nineteen-year-old and knocking out a reckless middle-aged multimillionaire. Even for me, this was stacking up to be a pretty bad day at the office.

"We need to get back on track," I said. "Let's grab some coffee and go over what we know so far."

The closest thing to a Starbucks we could find was a Greek diner across from the Bronx County Courthouse.

"We know from the Jacob Dunning abduction that our kidnapper hired illegals to purchase cell phones for him. Do you think he could have used yet another middleman—this Mark guy—to subcontract the money pickup?"

"It's possible, I guess," Parker said. "Though from all indications, our unsub seems to be more of a loner. But then again, the more I think about it, the more it sort of makes sense that maybe this was about money. He kills the first two as a calling card to prove to Hastings's father that he's dealing with a stone-cold maniac. Maybe from this point, we should go on the assumption that Hastings was the real target."

My aching neck actually made a cracking sound as I rolled it. I finally stood.

"Maybe you're right. Let's head back to Columbia."

Chapter 53

FROM THE THIRTIETH Precinct, we headed directly over to Dan Hastings's residence hall at Columbia. Because of his disability or maybe because of his father's connections, Dan Hastings had scored a room at the new dorm on 118th, which was otherwise reserved for law students. One of the Public Safety guys keyed us into his suite.

It was neat as a pin. There were some very expensive-looking custom furniture pieces and a closet full of clothes from stratosphere-priced Barneys. Beside the bed, we found copies of the *National Review* and the latest Sean Hannity book. Even Dan's sixty-inch plasma was tuned to the Fox News Channel.

"A closet conservative at Columbia? How do you like that?" Emily said.

As we watched, a report about the Mardi Gras celebration down in New Orleans started. I remembered the forehead ashes on the bodies of Jacob Dunning and Chelsea Skinner and the references to Ash Wednesday. Even though this was starting to look like an elaborate kidnapping-for-ransom plot, I couldn't completely shake the feeling that the three kidnappings were still related to this somehow.

Back down at the security desk, we got the cell number for Hastings's neighbor in the adjoining suite. We called and arranged to meet the first-year law student, Kenny Gruber, outside the gym, where he was playing basketball.

"Wheelchair or not, Dan was superpopular," Gruber said between chugs of his Red Bull. "He had more friends than anyone I know. He tossed incredible parties. Did you speak to Galina?"

"Who's that?" Emily said.

"His girlfriend, Galina Nesser. My God, is she hot. A Russian goddess. And a physics major. See what I mean about Dan being a unique dude? I mean, how does a guy in a wheelchair score a quality piece of ass like that?"

"A-hem," Emily coughed exaggeratedly.

"Oh, sorry, ma'am. Forgot my manners there," Gruber said. "You want to know more about Dan, you should talk to Galina."

" 'Ma'am'?" Emily said as we headed for the nearest campus exit. "Do I look like a ma'am to you?"

"Of course not," I said. "You look like a quality piece of—"

I sidestepped as Agent Parker punched me in the arm.

"What was that for?" I said, rubbing it. "I was merely going to say you look like a quality peace officer. Jeez, what did you think I was going to say?"

Chapter 54

FRANCIS X. MOONEY cursed under his breath as his taxi crested the 115th Street rise on Lenox Avenue. Down the low valley toward 125th Street and back up again on the other side, it was nothing but bumper-to-bumper red brake lights for another fifteen blocks.

He stuffed a twenty through the greasy partition's slot and popped the door latch. He was running unbelievably late. He'd have to hoof it.

He broke into a run as he hit the sidewalk. Christ, what a day, he thought as sweat began to pour down his face. He had so many balls in the air, he could hardly keep count.

He got to 137th Street without a minute to spare.

He was headed to the apartment of the death-row inmate Reginald Franklin's mother. Even with all his plans and all his incredibly important work, his conscience wouldn't let him forget the doomed man.

Off Lenox Avenue, down from the Harlem Hospital Center, he entered the battered front door of a narrow three-story brick tenement. The barking started the second he stepped through the open inner door and into a rancid-smelling stairwell.

No wonder Kurt from New York Heart had been reluctant to follow up on the case, he thought, listening to the unbelievably loud barks. No matter. Dogs or no dogs, someone's life was at stake here.

The door to Mrs. Franklin's second-floor apartment cracked open when Francis X. made the landing. He froze as an enormous dog lunged out of the apartment. It looked like a monster. It was a Presa Canario, the same breed of unbelievably vicious dog that had mauled a woman to death in San Francisco. It had a brindled coat and had to weigh close to 150 pounds.

Francis X. started breathing again only when he saw that there was a taut chain around its neck. It was being clutched by a wiry old black woman.

"I'm from New York Heart, ma'am," Francis said quickly. "The lawyer advocacy group? I'm here about your son, Reggie. I'd like to try to help him get a stay of execution. Could you please put up your pet, ma'am?"

"You got any ID, white boy?" she said between the ear-splitting barks.

Francis showed her his card from the social services agency. The dog snapped for it, almost swallowing it along with Francis's hand.

"Okay, okay. Just a second," the old woman finally said.

Was it him, or did the old African American woman have a smirk on her face?

"You said you was coming, too, right? Must have forgot. Sit tight till I get Chester back in the closet."

The door shut and opened again. The sound of Chester going absolutely batshit came from the rear of the apartment.

"C'mon in, I guess," she said, waving impatiently. "Close the damn door behind you. What did you say about Reggie?"

He followed her into the living room. *Judge Judy* was on the TV. The woman lay down on a couch and put up her feet. She didn't lower the volume.

"Well? What you want?"

"I heard about Reginald's latest denial, and I've gone to the liberty of writing up a request of stay to the governor. It's all done. I just need you to sign it. Then I'll take it to FedEx. A friend of mine from law school is in the Florida State Legislature, and though he can't guarantee anything, he is going to personally advocate for Reggie. I think we have a real good shot."

"I gotta pay?" Mrs. Franklin said as she motioned for him to bring her the paper.

"For my legal services? Of course not, Mrs. Franklin."

"No, I know *that,*" she said as she scratched her signature. "I meant for the FedEx. That shit's expensive."

"No, that's covered, too, of course."

"Good," she said with another little smirk. "Anything else?"

How about a fucking thank-you? Francis X. thought, unable to control his anger. Then he looked around the room. It wasn't her fault, he realized. Abject poverty made people this way. Mrs. Franklin was a victim, like her son.

"That's all," Francis said. "I'd better get going. Helping you and your son is my pleasure. It's the least I could do."

Chapter 55

IT WAS COMING on five when I had Emily drop me off at my apartment. The end-of-day task force meeting downtown at headquarters had been bumped up to six-thirty, and I was in desperate need of a shower and a change of clothes. I wasn't looking forward to the meeting. They would be looking to blame someone for the missing five million.

Inside, I grabbed a suit fresh from the dry cleaners from the front hall closet. It's always been a policy of mine to make sure to look my best when I'm going to be called on the carpet.

"It can't be, but it is! Daddy's home before dinner! Ahhhhh!" one of my daughters, Fiona, shrieked ecstatically as I appeared in the dining room doorway.

The gang, still in their school uniforms, were home from school and in the midst of getting their homework out of the way. I went around, slapping high fives and administering hugs and even a few atomic tickles where appropriate.

Many cops I've worked with have asked me why the hell I would want so many kids, and I've always had trouble explaining it. Yes, there are fights. Legendary lines for the bathroom. Clutter beyond the nightmares of professional organizers. Not to mention the expense. I envy people who can live paycheck to paycheck. But it's moments like these, when my guys are all safe and happy and busy and together, that every bit of it is incredibly worth it, when it is pure, unabashed happiness.

The kids are simply my tribe, my pack. We gathered them together, and everything good that my wife, Maeve, and I had ever learned, we passed on to them. Not only have they taken those lessons to heart in our house—being kind to one another, being polite, being good even when they don't feel like it—as they get older, they've started spreading that goodness to the world. I can't count how many times teachers and neighbors and school parents have said to me how wonderful, polite, and thoughtful they thought my kids were.

Maeve, and now Mary Catherine, being home with them every day, could take ninety-nine percent of the credit for that. But that one percent that makes me proud of myself exceeds everything I have ever accomplished professionally, hands down.

Mary Catherine smiled up at me from where she was surrounded by a sea of blue-and-gold Catholic-school plaid.

"Mike, is it you?" she said. "Can I fix dinner?"

"Don't bother," I said, putting my cell on the sideboard as I headed for my room. "This is just a pit stop. I have an hour, maybe less, until this evil object summons me again."

Twenty minutes later, wearing a suit not covered in sweat, antifreeze, and grass stains, I stepped back into the dining room and almost fainted. Instead of being covered in textbooks, workbooks, red pens, calculators, and rulers, the table was set like it was Sunday all over again.

Mary Catherine and Brian and Juliana came in a second later with a plate of homemade fried chicken, jalapeño corn bread, and a fresh salad. Another incredible meal brought to you by my personal savior, Mary Catherine.

I shook my head at her for going to all the trouble.

Besides my wife, Mary Catherine was the most genuinely generous person I'd ever met.

Who knew? Maybe this meant she was even a little less pissed at me.

After we said our prayers, I wolfed down a piece of hot corn bread. I closed my eyes in ecstasy.

"How can an Irish girl do Southern cooking this well?" I said, spraying crumbs. "Let me guess, you're from the southwest part of Ireland?"

The smiles and happy, fuzzy mood all popped like a cigarette on a balloon when my blasted phone rang. I was standing up to get it when Chrissy reached back and grabbed it.

"Oh, no, Daddy," she said, tossing it across the table to Bridget. "You're staying right here. No phone means no work."

They actually started chanting, "No phone! No work!" as our game of Monkey in the Middle began. Guess who the monkey was.

"That's not funny, guys," I said, trying not to laugh and failing.

I also failed to get to the phone. A game of Monkey in the Middle really isn't fair against ten people. Eleven, actually, as Mary pretended to offer it to me and then passed it behind her back to the waiting Brian. He tossed it to Eddie, who opened it.

"I'm sorry, but Mr. Bennett is not available," Eddie said as everyone cracked up. "Please leave your name at the sound of the beep. Beep!"

"Mike, is that you?" Emily said as I finally wrested it from him.

"Sorry about that, Parker. My family is being funny. At least they think they are. What's up?"

"One guess," she said.

"No," I said.

"Yes," she said grimly. "Another kid was grabbed, Mike. I'm pulling up in front of your building right now."

Chapter 56

EMILY HANDED ME her notes on the latest kidnapping as I buckled myself into the passenger seat of her Fedmobile. She surprised me by having a piping-hot black venti in my drink holder and a black-and-white cookie from Zaro's on the dash. I noticed she was also doing a pretty professional job of carving our way south through the chaos of midtown Manhattan dinner traffic.

Unhealthy food and a healthy dose of road rage, I thought with an impressed nod. My new partner was getting this New York cop thing down pretty fast.

The calm from my shower and my visit with the kids lasted less than a New York minute as I scanned the pages of her notes. The latest victim was the youngest yet: a seventeen-year-old high school student named Mary Beth Haas. She'd been missing since noon. She'd last been spotted leaving the very exclusive all-girls Brearley School on East 83rd Street to go to the school's gym on East 87th. She'd never made it there. The poor teenage girl seemed to have disappeared into thin air.

"The similarity to the Hastings kidnapping is striking," I said. "Both were grabbed from exclusive Manhattan schools. We need to check for teaching staff who have a history in both places."

"No new leads on Hastings?" Emily inquired.

"Some Twenty-sixth Precinct squad guys are out looking for the Russian girlfriend, but so far nothing," I said as I looked back down at the report.

I read that Mary Beth Haas's mother, Ann, was the CEO and main shareholder in the Price Templeton Fund, the second-largest mutual fund on Wall Street. No wonder our newest case had loudly rung every alarm bell down at One Police Plaza.

"I Googled the mother," Emily said. "She's, like, the fifth- or sixth-richest woman in the country. Her father started the fund, but they said she worked herself up from an analyst and probably would have ended up as CEO even if she hadn't been left thirty-four percent of the stock in her dad's will. She's also one of the largest contributors to the New York Philharmonic and Public Library."

"Another only child of an A-list mega-wealthy New Yorker, like the Dunnings, the Skinners, and Gordon Hastings?" I asked.

Emily nodded. "I can't believe he's hit another one so fast. He actually had to have grabbed Mary Beth before we did the money exchange for Hastings."

"For the love of God," I said, wanting to punch something. "I thought he'd be done after getting his five million. Now two in one day? What is this guy made of? And what the hell is he after if it's not money?"

We shot over the Brooklyn Bridge and pulled off the first exit into the borough's most exclusive neighborhood of Brooklyn Heights. Two undercover cars were already parked in front of the Haases' stately Greek Revival brownstone on a tree-lined street called Columbia Heights. It overlooked the Brooklyn Promenade and had, perhaps, the most majestic view of lower Manhattan that exists.

A female detective I knew from Brooklyn South Homicide answered the door. Behind her, a task force techie in an NYPD Geek Squad Windbreaker was taking apart a wall phone.

I looked up as a petite fiftyish woman with very

short blond hair came down the stairs. She kept passing a hand back obsessively through her hair as she spoke rapidly into a cell phone. I groaned inwardly at the intense sorrow and despair on Ann Haas's face. I could only imagine what she was going through. Could only guess how unimaginably sad and angry and destroyed I'd feel if one of my kids were missing. Mrs. Haas was a woman who was most definitely going through hell.

"I think the FBI's here now, John. I'll call you back," the distraught mother said into the cell as she arrived at the bottom of the stairs. She waved us into the living room.

Her dropped cell phone clattered off an antique oak steamer trunk she used as a coffee table as she collapsed back onto a huge, silk-upholstered coach. Despite her expensive power suit, when she pulled her black-hose-clad legs up underneath her, she suddenly looked like a little girl. A little girl who'd lost her only doll, I thought to myself.

The high-def night skyline of lower Manhattan seemed to scratch up against the glass of the bay window behind her. She turned and stared at the office towers.

"I took us out of that insane place in order to provide some sort of normalcy and security after Mary

Beth was born," she said quietly as she shook her head. "I wanted to send her to and from Brearley by car, but ever since Mary Beth was fourteen, she's insisted on taking the subway.

"I have friends who hire professionals to try to get their wealthy kids to understand how normal people live, but it was almost the opposite with Mary Beth. It was like pulling teeth every time I had to convince her that it was okay to use the resources we've been fortunate enough to acquire."

She looked at me, perplexed, as if I might know the answer to the affliction she was now suffering from. It pissed me off that I didn't.

"Is your husband here?" I said.

"He works for UBS in London during the week, but he's on the next plane back. Did you know some fool at Brearley actually tried to tell me my daughter might have just cut class? Mary Beth is the captain of both the lacrosse and volleyball teams. She got an early acceptance to Bard, for the love of God. This is not a girl who cuts classes.

"Please tell me you have an idea of who this person is who might have taken her. Please tell me you're going to bring my Mary Beth back home."

The woman's hurt eyes locked on mine again as she started to silently weep. They only tore away as

Emily sat down next to the woman and laid a hand on her wrist.

"We'll do everything possible, Mrs. Haas," Emily said. "I can't guarantee you anything except that we'll go to the ends of the earth to bring your little girl home again."

Chapter 57

DESPITE ANN HAAS'S obvious pain, she managed to tell Emily and me about her daughter, Mary Beth. She was a solid 4.0 student whose dream was to help the poor of Latin America, where she'd summered from the time she was fourteen at various volunteer camps.

"This year, instead of going to Europe like a lot of her friends, Mary Beth is planning to run a children's theater in Pérez Zeledón, one of the poorest sections of Costa Rica," the CEO told us as she handed us a picture. "It's all she can talk about."

Mary Beth was a slightly overweight, attractive, blue-eyed girl with long jet-black hair. In the picture, she was wearing a green bandanna and matching camo shirt and cargo shorts as she smiled and waved from some muddy jungle path.

Most surprising of all to me was that Mary Beth didn't have a social networking account on either MySpace or Facebook, unlike the other victims. A throwback, I thought, looking at her smile. A very good and special kid.

Ann Haas was about to take us up to her daughter's room, when her wall phone rang. The department geek set up by the fireplace glanced at his laptop and nodded vigorously. I motioned for Mrs. Haas to pick up the phone in the family room as the tech handed me a set of headphones.

Mrs. Haas's knuckles were as bloodless as her face as she lifted the cordless phone.

"Yes?" she said.

"Mrs. Haas," the kidnapper said. "Poor, poor Mrs. Haas. How ironic, considering the latest *Forbes* listing, wouldn't you say?"

I nodded to everyone around the room. It was the same guy.

"Oh, Mrs. Haas," the kidnapper continued. "How glorious you look at your charity events. How brightly the flash packs of the paparazzi reflect off your diamonds. While the lights dazzled, did you maybe for a moment think that you had become more than

BPA/BPS Free

Recyclable

Sustainably Sourced

This receipt helps

#200 01-02-2024 11:28AM
Item(s) checked out to p47514474.

TITLE: Worst case [large print]
BRCD: 35922002557803
DUE DATE: 01-30-24

mortal? I think you did. Pride is one of your main sins, Ann. I can call you Ann, can't I? I hope you don't mind. After spending so much time with your daughter, I feel like we're practically related."

"You fucking prick son of a bitch!" Mrs. Haas screamed. "Give her back!"

The kidnapper let out a long, sad sigh.

"My, my. What filth even a daughter of the highest privilege is capable of in our tainted society. Is that really any way to talk? Did those tight-ass lily-white-tower academics teach you to speak like that at Sarah Lawrence? Or did you learn that potty mouth at Daddy's trading desk? Mustn't we have been turned on, being one of the few women amongst all that heady Wall Street warrior testosterone?

"Which leads us to your next sin, Ann. Lust. Multiple acts of adultery with multiple partners, if the rumors are true. Shall I get into specifics?

"Isn't that what being rich is all about? Sex and money and hiring people to clean the eight-hundred-thread-count sheets? You're a filthy sinner, Ann, and so's your lackluster English poseur of a husband."

"Please let me speak to Mary Beth," Mrs. Haas begged. "Just for a second. For whatever I've done to you, I'm sorry."

"So am I," the kidnapper said. "But talking to

Mary Beth won't be possible. I'm here to teach you that you are human, Ann. And like all humans, you must come to terms with the reality of loss. Sin and loss go hand in hand. Please put my friend Detective Bennett on the phone now. It's been a real pleasure speaking to you, despite your disgusting language. I hope he hasn't pumped up your hopes concerning Mary Beth, Madam Chief Executive. On second thought, I hope he has. All the more pride to goeth before the fall. Ta-ta."

"Detective Bennett here," I said, taking the phone from the weeping CEO. "How's Mary Beth? Is she okay?"

"Mary Beth is fine, Mike. For now. She has a big test coming up, though. A *final* final, you might say. It's all in her hands. I'll call you back the second her score is tallied."

"Wait a minute. Don't you want money?"

"All the money on this earth couldn't prevent Mary Beth from facing her destiny, Mike."

What the hell did that mean? How did that make sense? There was a sharp sound in the background suddenly, a distinctive *click-clack*. I winced. Goddammit. He'd just chambered an automatic pistol.

"Pray for her, Mike. That's all she has now."

Chapter 58

MARY BETH HAAS bit harder into the thick wraps of gauze gagged into her mouth as she wrestled herself up into a cramped seated position.

She was in a pitch-black metal box with a low lid and cold, rusty walls and floor. Her arms were tightly wrapped around herself in a straitjacket. She'd been in the box for several hours. At first she'd been terrified. Then angry. Now she was just sad, infinitely, inconsolably, hopelessly sad.

As she sat in the cramped dark, the events of the afternoon kept playing and replaying through her mind in a nightmare loop.

She knew she wasn't really allowed to leave campus to run laps at the Brearley Field House on 87th, but since she was a senior and the cocaptain of the reigning New York State Championship volleyball team, her teachers and her coach often looked the other way when she snuck out during her morning free period.

She had been coming through one of those cave-like construction scaffolding tunnels across the street from the gym when a man standing beside the open door of a van had said, "Mary Beth?"

She remembered a stinging numbness in her chest as she turned toward the voice. Her whole entire body seemed to cramp at once as she fell forward, powerless. A strong, wet, medicinal smell filled her nose and mouth then, and she was out.

She'd woken up in the straitjacket with a massive headache. That had been what? Seven? Maybe eight hours before? Eight hours of blackness and silence. Eight hours of being starving and thirsty and dirty and having to use the bathroom. It was like she was stuck at sea. A sea of darkness where there seemed to be no hope of being rescued.

At first, the sadness had been sharp, but now it was lessening, weakening like a candle dying out. She thought of her friends and teachers. Her mom. I'm sorry, everyone, she thought. Sorry for being so stupid. Sorry for messing up.

She didn't know how much more time had elapsed when she heard the clacking of a steel shutter rolling up.

Oh, God! Somebody was coming. The man who had taken her.

An unhinging bolt of animal panic gripped her, froze her. He would touch her now, wouldn't he? That's what they did, right? Crazy men? Hurt you. Raped you. Killed you. She whimpered. It would be better just to be buried. She didn't want to be in pain.

That's when she shook herself out of her pity. She found a hard place inside herself and went there. She would fight for her life. She would bite and scream and kick. She found the thought of it comforting. She wanted to live, but more than that, she wanted to fight. She suddenly knew she could, and that was somehow better.

There was the sound of a car motor approaching. The *clackety-clack* of a metal gate going back down again. The killing of the engine and the sound of the door opening made her new strength waver for a moment, but then she bit down harder on the gag, and it was back.

I want to live, she thought. Please, God, just allow me the chance to live.

Chapter 59

THE METALLIC SCRAPE of a lock was loud right next to Mary Beth's ear. The lid of the steel box screeched as it opened.

Even in the poor light, she knew it was him. The suit. The gray hair and the glasses. He looked intelligent, fatherly, like a kindly doctor or a popular professor. How could men be so evil? she thought.

Her arms and especially her hands were strong from volleyball. He'd free her to get at her, wouldn't he? First chance she got, she'd smash the side of her fist into his glasses, try to ram a shard into his eye as deep as it would go.

He lifted her out by the straps on the back of her jacket. She saw that she'd been held in a large industrial toolbox. They were in an enormous dark warehouse of some kind. Behind the van were girderlike pillars and welding gas tanks. Could she kick one over and start a fire? Best of all was a high window above the steel shutter of the door. The world lay on its other side.

Make it there, she urged herself. For everything that everyone in your life has done for you, make it there.

The man sat her on a bench beside a metal table and sat down on the other side of it.

He took two items out of his jacket pockets and laid them on the tabletop for her to see. She made another whimper at the sight of them.

They were a straight razor and a black pistol.

"I'm going to remove your gag. If you scream, I'm going to have to cut up that flawless face of yours, Mary Beth. Nod if you understand."

She nodded. He leaned across the table, slid the cold flat of the razor to her cheek, and shredded the gauze. She breathed through her mouth as she worked her sore jaw, wishing her hands were free to scratch her cheeks.

"Hi, Mary Beth," he said. "Do you know who I am?"

Um, let me guess, she thought. You're the sick freak who's going around killing rich teenagers?

"The man from the paper. The one the police are looking for," she said instead.

He nodded, grinned.

"Guilty as charged," he said. "I won't lie to you. The people who have died so far have done so because they failed a test. We no longer have the luxury in this world to allow those who are unworthy to live. That's why I have brought you here. I need to find out if *you* are worthy."

A test, Mary Beth thought as the man rolled and then lit a cigarette. As he exhaled blue fragrant smoke from his nose, she allowed herself a tiny sliver of hope. She suspected that he was lying, just playing games with her, but if he wasn't, maybe she could pull this off.

If anything, she was smart. She'd gotten a 2120 on her SAT, been early accepted to Bard, her first choice. Most kids she knew came up with a whole bunch of bull crap for their college applications, but hers, all her volunteering and extracurricular activities, were actually true. She really did love to learn and read and engage her mind.

Please let it be true, she thought.

He tapped some ash on the table between the razor blade and the gun.

"Okay, question one: Tell me about fair trade

coffee prices and their effect on South American coffee growers."

Oh, my God, Mary Beth thought excitedly. I actually know this. It was last month's topic from her Political Awareness committee at school.

"The modern fair trade movement began in 'eighty-eight in Holland," she said. "It came about because of the horrendous exploitation of the Southern Hemisphere field-workers. It's basically an economic partnership that protects small coffee growers and gives consumers a choice to pay a little more for their joe while providing a living wage for the workers. The summer I was fifteen, I actually went on a fair harvest trip to Nicaragua."

For a moment, it looked like the cigarette was going to drop from the gray-haired man's lower lip. He recovered quickly.

"You're right," he said, taking a drag. "Now let's shift gears to global warming. How many gallons of gasoline are consumed by Americans each year?"

"One hundred forty-six billion gallons," Mary Beth said without hesitation. She knew this answer because of the mock United Nations project she'd completed at school. She'd been given the role of representative from Darfur on their global-energy-issues debate.

For the first time, the man with the gray hair seemed to genuinely smile. He crushed his cigarette under his shoe. He even took the razor off the table and put it back into his pocket.

"Correct again," he said. "That's good, Mary Beth. You're doing well. So far, at least. But we have many more questions to get through. Now, question three. The subject: abject hunger in the world's richest nation."

Chapter 60

WE SAT THERE, staring at the phone. It just didn't make sense. The kidnapper should have called back by now. Every other time, he'd called to let us know where the body was. Was not telling us and leaving the parents hanging his latest method of torture? If it was, it was working like a charm.

The only whiff of a lead came when Verizon Wireless called back with a cell site triangulation of his first call. It had come from somewhere in the vicinity of Gateway National Beach, on the south shore of Staten Island. But not surprisingly, when detectives from the 122nd Precinct had raced to the scene, they found nothing but gulls. The killer could have been in a car when he'd called—or who knew? A boat maybe. Another stone wall. Another dead end.

When I went to the window for about the thirtieth time, I noticed a funny thing happening on the sidewalk out in front of the Haases' brownstone. A crowd had formed. It looked like a block party.

I went outside, thinking at first it was the press, but then I spotted a Brearley sweatshirt. Mary Beth's friends. They were holding candles beside a pile of teddy bears and flowers and a signed volleyball. Almost every member of the Brearley senior class showed up to the vigil. They were crying, smoking, holding pictures of her.

I thought about breaking it up but then decided, why? If the kidnapper was watching the house, maybe the outpouring of love might make him see Mary Beth as a flesh-and-blood valuable person instead of the symbol of his hate.

I stared at the young, solemn faces as a guitar started playing. The vigil was oddly beautiful. The flickering flames from the candles seemed to merge with the lights of Manhattan across the dark bay. Mary Beth was obviously a great kid who had affected many lives.

It set my teeth on edge that I couldn't find her.

Even after all this time, we were as baffled by everything as anyone, completely useless.

Ann Haas came outside and was embraced by her daughter's friends. She ordered pizza. Emily and I joined her in handing it out. I have to say, I was pretty overwhelmed by the emotional reactions of everyone, the genuine outreaching to comfort one another. Too bad it so often has to take tragedy to bring out the best in people, I thought.

Emily and I used the opportunity to learn more about Mary Beth. Ann Haas introduced me to Kevin Adello, a tall, mop-headed basketball player from Collegiate, Brearley's exclusive brother school. He told us he'd dated Mary Beth off and on.

"She's going to Bard, and instead of going to Princeton, I decided to go play for Vassar so we could be near each other. She isn't like any other girl at Brearley, I'll tell you that. Mary Beth is real. She'd puke seeing all these debutantes here in their just-so Seven jeans. I'm sorry. I'm being too harsh. I guess it's nice that they showed. I just wish I could do something."

I wheeled around as a cab slowed in the street. The crowd converged on it. My blood went cold as a ragged cry rang out.

"Move!" I yelled as I forced shocked teenagers aside.

A scared-looking girl in a wrinkled Brearley hoodie opened the door of the cab as I arrived beside it.

"It's okay," Mary Beth said, holding her hands up. "I'm okay."

What? I couldn't believe it. Another twist. The first one in the case that was actually welcome. Mary Beth's bowled-over friends clapped and whistled as I guided her toward the brownstone stairs and her joyfully crying mother.

He'd let Mary Beth live?

Chapter 61

BACK INSIDE UNDER the kitchen high hats, Emily and I stood back as the mother and daughter embraced. I couldn't tell which of them was crying the hardest. It even looked like Emily was about to join in.

"Something in your eye there, Detective Badass?" she teased.

"Hey," I whispered to her, blinking back the moistness. "I guess I must have a heart or something, huh? You breathe a word about it to Schultz or Ramirez, we'll be exchanging gunfire."

"Toss me a block now, Mike," Emily said, taking a deep breath. "We need to debrief the girl while she's still fresh. I need to get Mary Beth alone."

"Mrs. Haas? Can I talk to you for a moment?"

I said, tapping the mother on the arm. "We need to start thinking about a media strategy. It's very important."

"Now?" she said as I ushered her into the hall. "Can't it wait? I have to get my daughter cleaned up now. She needs me. Nothing is more important than that. In fact, why are you still here? I'd like you to leave so we can all get back to normal."

"Mom!" Mary Beth yelled. It was the first time she'd spoken since she'd come inside. "They need to talk to me. Is that so insane? Ugggh. Stop treating me like I'm three. I'm fine."

Ann Haas's eyes widened in surprise as I was finally able to get her out into the hall. I was starting to like the feisty teen more by the minute. Emily began questioning the girl.

"Hi, Mary Beth. My name is Emily Parker. I work with the FBI. I can't tell you how happy we are that you're okay. But right now, I need you to answer some questions to see if we can catch the person who abducted you."

"If you're going to give me a speech about rape kits and stuff, don't bother. He didn't touch me."

"Good. That's very good. In that case, Mary Beth, can you describe him? How old is he? What does he look like?"

"He's in his late fifties maybe. Broad-shouldered, about six feet tall. He has salt-and-pepper hair. He's actually pretty handsome. He reminded me of that actor, the father from *The Day After Tomorrow*. Dennis Quaid. Only paler and with glasses. He also wore an expensive suit."

Parker scribbled it down. Why wouldn't this guy wear a mask or something if he was going to let her go? she thought. Was it sloppiness? Another trick?

"He's actually not that bad a guy," Mary Beth continued. "I know it sounds weird, but he cares about stuff. Probably too much. After everything, I guess I feel sorry for him more than anything else."

What?

"How do you mean?" Parker said instead.

"He gave me a list of questions about the horrible direction this world is headed in. Like a test, I guess. Every correct answer I gave made him happier and happier. He was actually crying at the end. He told me how proud he was of me. Told me to try to learn everything I could at Bard. Said that the world was really going to need me. He apologized for having put me through the whole thing and then he drove me to a corner and put me in a cab. He even paid the cabbie."

Parker had to use effort not to shake her head in bafflement. This guy really was nuts.

"You didn't happen to get his plate?"

"No," she said. "It was a light-colored van. Yellow, I think."

"Anything else at all, Mary Beth?"

"He hand-rolls his own cigarettes. He made a cross with the ashes on my forehead right before he let me out. Look," she said, reaching up to touch it.

Parker grabbed her wrist tightly as the girl went to wipe it off.

"Mike! Get in here!" she yelled triumphantly. "I think we got a print!"

Chapter 62

BECAUSE WE DIDN'T have time to wait for the Crime Scene Unit to arrive, we lifted the print ourselves. And when I say "we," I mean Emily.

I stayed with Mary Beth while Special Agent Parker went to the G car and came back with some surgical gloves and 3M fingerprint tape.

"This will just take a second, hon," Emily said as she laid the tape meticulously across the teen's forehead. With a light, deft motion, Emily flattened out the tape and peeled off the print.

I had to contain a whoop as she laid the tape on the white fingerprint card. It was perfect. Even taking a print off a pane of cold glass can sometimes be difficult, but Emily had lifted this print as well as any CSU pro. Was there anything this Bureau chick couldn't do?

Afterward, we headed back to the G car's trunk, and Emily took out a large gray box. It was a LiveScan 10 printer, a portable fingerprint scanning machine. She connected it to the Fed car's Mobile Computer Terminal and with one small scan, the print was fired down to the FBI's Integrated Automated Fingerprint Identification System in Clarksburg, West Virginia.

If our boy's prints were among the fifty million the IAFIS contained, we'd get a response within two hours. This was by far our best lead yet. I was stoked.

"We need to get this down to the lab in DC as well for synchrotron infrared microspectroscopy," Emily said, dropping the print card into an evidence envelope.

"A syncro infra what?" I said.

"It's brand-new. See, in every print there's little traces of sweat. The lab techs can now look at the sweat and detect chemical markers. The markers reveal whether a suspect uses drugs and even detect the hormones that indicate the suspect's sex. If we don't obtain a hit on the print, we need to obtain as much info as we can. You're telling me you never heard of it?"

"Of course I've heard of it. Are you kidding me?" I lied. "I just wanted to see if you knew."

Chapter 63

MARY BETH WAS sitting down with the just-arrived police sketch artist when we left the brownstone. That's when I noticed that the crowd outside the Haases' had changed. The teenagers looked much more vicious, heartless, almost hyenalike. Oh, I thought, spotting a news van. That explains it.

I was scanning for a slot to get through the converging newsies, when I suddenly stopped at the town house's bottom step. Instead of running, I waved the crowd toward me. I had an idea.

"I have an announcement," I said.

I cleared my throat as lights and microphones leaned toward me. Peering at me from behind the bulky cameras and apparatus, the surrounding press people looked like an invading army of alien cyborgs. The problem I had with them was that they often treated me like I was part of an invading army of alien cyborgs.

"Today another young victim was abducted, but this one was released unharmed," I began. "First off, if the person responsible is listening, I want to thank them for their mercy in this case. I would also urge them strongly to contact me so that we might be able to resolve this situation once and for all. I'm available anytime day or night. You have my number. Please do not hesitate to speak with me."

"Do you have any leads in the case?" one of the cyborgs called to me.

"Goddammit," I said angrily. "Can't you see we have an investigation to run? That's it now. Out of my way. I mean it!"

Parker was silent as we stepped to the car. Then she suddenly snapped her fingers.

"Oh, I see," she said. "You wanted to get the pissed-off-cop routine on the eleven-o'clock news. You're trying to make our guy think we're still running around in circles instead of getting closer."

"Exactly," I said with a wink. "Why let on that we're getting closer to grabbing him? That'll only make him run. I need to make him think that he's still way ahead of us. Then *bam!* Once we get this fingerprint hit, we nail him cold."

"That's brilliant, Mike," Emily said. "I love it."

"Hey," I said. "I'm just trying to keep up with you, Special Agent."

I checked my watch.

"I just hope to God he hasn't done that Hastings kid yet. We need that hit fast. And if that's not enough to worry about, it'll be Ash Wednesday in a few hours. Who knows what this loon has planned."

"Maybe he's cut us some slack and decided to head to New Orleans to catch the tail end of Mardi Gras," Emily said.

"Sounds like fun," I said. "You and I should go, too. I could use a road trip."

"Not so fast, Mike. If all goes well, we'll have the ID of the kidnapper in an hour and a half. After we put this lunatic out of business, I'll buy the first round."

Chapter 64

LIMOUSINES AND TOWN cars were three deep out in front of the Waldorf Astoria as Francis Mooney stepped north up Park Avenue. He had to walk in the street to avoid the scrum of paparazzi stuffed behind sidewalk barricades. He was temporarily blinded as a limo door popped open and three dozen flash packs went off at once. A scruffy young man in a tuxedo emerged, squinting merrily in the brilliant shower of white light. An actor perhaps?

The American Refugee Committee was having its benefit tonight, Francis remembered, putting the scene at his back. He was happy that ARC was having such a stunning turnout. Mooney had been on the organization's board ten years ago and knew it to be a terrific organization, unlike the many charities whose bloated CEO salaries and outrageous benefits budgets soaked up most of the donations.

Continuing up Park, he thought about Mary Beth Haas. He cursed himself for the thousandth time for not wearing a mask during the test. He'd been positive she was going to fail. He'd gotten lazy, and someone had seen his face. Oh, well. Couldn't worry about it now. Places to go, he thought.

Three minutes later, he quickly turned the corner onto 52nd and passed beneath the awning of the legendary Four Seasons restaurant on the north side of the street. Coming up the stairs, he smiled at a startling black-haired woman in a gravity-defying backless gown who was speaking German into a cell phone. More chic women and slim, suited men waited for their tables beneath the Picasso inside. He inhaled the expensive-perfume-thick air. Cedar, gardenia, ambrette, he thought with a sigh. Now, that's what money smells like.

The sleek, platinum-haired maître d', Cristophe, rushed toward him from the front bar.

"Mr. Mooney," he said with a flourished raising of his hands. "Finally, you have arrived. Mrs. Clautier was worried. May I take your coat?"

"Thank you so much, Cristophe," Mooney said,

allowing him to remove his camel hair as the rest of the elegant crowd pretended not to gape at his royal treatment.

"Has she been waiting long?"

"Not so long, Mr. Mooney. Shall I take your case as well?"

Francis hefted the briefcase with the 9-millimeter Beretta in it, as if debating.

"You know what, Cristophe? I might as well hold on to it."

He stopped for a moment before he followed the maître d' into the restaurant's storied Pool Room. He took in the glittering white-marble center pool, the shimmering chain-link drapes, the important and beautiful people at the crisp, glowing tables, all eating with a meticulous casualness. He could almost feel the power thrumming through the floor. Even he couldn't deny that the sensation was exhilarating.

The other board members of New York Restore had already arrived. They were seated at the double table by the pool that they always reserved for their quarterly dinner meeting.

"Well, if it isn't our wild Irish chairman," Mrs. Clautier said. "In all the time I've known you, Francis, I do believe this is the very first time you've ever been late."

"I can't tell you how hectic things have been at the office," Francis said, grinning widely as he kissed her Cartier-diamond-encrusted hand. "The important thing is, I'm here now to bask in the glow of your loveliness."

"Such a charmer," Mrs. Clautier said with a sigh as she touched his cheek. "Francis, as I've told you many a time, you were born several generations too late."

"And you several too early, my dear," Francis said. He declined the menu the tuxedoed waiter offered and ordered the Dover sole.

"I was with Caroline at lunch today, and she told me that Sloan-Kettering is doing celebrity-designed lunch boxes for their soiree," Mrs. Clautier told the group. "Isn't that a hoot? Brooke came up with the idea."

For Mrs. Clautier, diva of the New York social set, to actually go out of her way to supply the last names Kennedy and Shields would have been beneath her, Francis knew.

Mrs. Clautier was an unapologetic snob. In truth, he really couldn't give two shits about New York Restore and its insipid mission to maintain and beautify Manhattan's playgrounds and public spaces. The only reason he'd decided to head it was to humor the generous Mrs. Clautier. Over the years, he'd become a kind of unofficial philanthropy consultant to her, and he had been able to steer millions of the limitless oil fortune her husband had left her to other much more important causes.

In fact, he was going to squeeze her for the biggest amount he'd ever chanced right after the meal. The papers, all ready for her to sign, were under the holstered automatic in his briefcase.

"Champagne, Mr. Mooney?" the ever discreet table captain whispered to Francis as Mrs. Clautier's regaling veered into tales of the latest mischief her Pekingese, Charlie, had gotten into.

"Glenlivet. A double," Mooney whispered back.

Part Four

CHARITY CASE

Chapter 65

WAKING ABRUPTLY IN the dark, Francis Mooney immediately regretted the third Scotch he'd ordered the night before. Alcohol always disrupted his sleep. He was trying to fall back when the 1010 WINS xylophone started up from his radio alarm.

"Good morning," the anchor said. "It's five-thirty. Alternate side of the street parking is suspended today for Ash Wednesday."

Despair surged like vomit into the back of Francis's throat at the mention of the day.

It was here, he thought as he began to whimper inconsolably. No! It's too soon. I can't face this. How can I face doing this?

Tears poured down his cheeks. It took him a full

ten minutes of breathing slowly to control himself enough to sit up. He squeezed his fists, digging his fingernails into his palms as hard as he could. The pain was exquisite, but it did the trick. He wiped his eyes, shut off the radio, and swung his feet out of bed.

He made coffee and carried it through the immaculate rooms of his 25th Street Chelsea town house. Up a circular staircase on the second floor was his favorite place, his rooftop lounge.

Outside, the cold air was pleasant as he wiggled his bare toes on the tar paper. He remembered playing tag on the roof of his Inwood tenement when he was a child. Was that why he liked this rooftop lounge so much?

From the almost-empty street below, he heard a speeding cab's tire slap off a road plate. He smiled, looking north at the green McGraw-Hill Building, which loomed like some landlocked Art Deco cruise ship. His smile departed as he turned toward the hint of dawn on the dark eastern horizon behind the Empire State Building.

The day was coming. It would not be stopped. Another tear rolled down his cheek. He wiped it away. He finally steeled himself with a breath and tipped his mug at the coming dawn as if in a toast.

Gray light was spilling down 25th Street as

he locked his front door half an hour later. He always dressed well, but this morning of all mornings, he'd pulled out all the stops. He slid a hand down the sleek lapel of his best suit, a light gray chalk-stripe Henry Poole he'd splurged on when he was in London on business six years before. The thirty-two-hundred-dollar black John Lobb calfskin brogues on his feet complemented it perfectly. The only thing that didn't really go was the large case he carried. It was black and boxy with stainless-steel hasps.

He popped the cuffs of his Italian milled-poplin Turnbull & Asser shirt as he carefully lifted the heavy case and brought it with him out into the street to hail a taxi.

The church that the cab let him out in front of ten minutes later was Most Holy Redeemer on 3rd Street in the East Village. He'd chosen it as his parish because it was the city's most tolerant, catering to gays and the HIV-positive.

At the votive offering inside the tiny chapel, he lit some candles and said a prayer for the teenagers he had killed. Like martyrs', their souls would ascend directly to heaven, he knew. Their necessary sacrifice was most certainly acknowledged by God. Francis had faith in that. How could he have done this without faith?

He raised his head as the organ began. The seven-o'clock mass was about to start. He quickly lit a last candle.

"So that my faith will not waver this day, my Lord," he whispered in the scented darkness.

He sat in the last pew. When the time came, he lined up behind the dozen early churchgoers and got his ashes. They were made from palms like the ones that had welcomed the Lord on the last week of His life. Francis found comfort in that fact. The scratch of the priest's thumb on his forehead almost made him cry out. Then the sacred words of Latin were in his ears.

"Memento homo, quia pulvis es, et in pulverem reverteris."

Know that you are dust and to dust you shall return.

"I am dust," Francis said to himself as he turned and came back down the aisle. He felt amazing, unblemished, filled with the light of the Lord's grace. He scooped up the heavy valise he had left by the kneeler. His step was light as he came out of the church into the new morning.

Chapter 66

OUT ON THE sidewalk the next morning, despite my sleep deprivation, I found myself smiling as I walked my kids to church. Cutting an extra-wide swath through the bustling Manhattan foot traffic, Chrissy and Shawna entertained one and all by singing every Nationwide and free-credit-report-dot-com commercial they knew by heart.

Wearing their plaid school uniforms and walking in two sort of straight lines, my ten boys and girls looked like they'd stepped off the first page of *Madeline*. Maybe I wasn't as tough as Miss Clavel, but I did carry a Glock.

My gang's warmth and lack of self-consciousness as we walked were contagious enough that I almost forgot the horror of my latest case. That is, until we ran into the solemn people spilling out of the early mass at Holy Name.

My eyes locked on the ashes on their foreheads. My stomach churned as images of the two dead teens shot through my mind. I could almost see the blood patterns from their wounds on the church steps.

I let out an angry breath. It made me sick that something so holy had taken on such a twisted symbolism. Ashes were supposed to symbolize sacrifice and humbleness at Christ's suffering. They weren't supposed to be a detail in an autopsy report that I couldn't get out of my head.

The churchgoers themselves seemed a little self-conscious. Last night Seamus had told me that the archdiocese had done a little hand-wringing over whether to distribute ashes today, because of the high-profile case. I was glad wiser heads had prevailed down at St. Pat's. Having one person hold such sway over all of New York City's Catholics would have been horrendous.

As we entered the church, Eddie and Ricky headed toward the front to put on their altar boy attire. Julia led the rest of the kids into the church's rear pew as I went over to the votives.

I dropped a five into the offering box and lit

candles. Kneeling down before their ruby glow, I closed my eyes and said prayers for the dead and most especially for their families. I knew all too well how completely devastating death could be in a tight-knit family. I could only guess at a parent's depth of despair that the loss of an only child would bring.

As I was crossing myself, I felt a tap on my shoulder. It was Seamus.

"Good man. Just the lad I was looking for," he whispered. "I need a volunteer. Will you do the first reading or bring up the gifts? Your choice."

"Bring up the gifts," I said.

"Actually, you'll have to do both. I lied about that choice thing. Let's get this show on the road."

The mass seemed more solemn and sadder than usual. Try as I might, I couldn't get the killer out of my thoughts even when Seamus whispered the High Latin phrase used on this solemn holy day.

"Memento homo, quia pulvis es, et in pulverem reverteris," he said as he administered the ashes.

From dust we are born and to dust we shall return, I thought. It was the same thing written on the blackboard next to the first poor young man's corpse.

Please, God, help me to stop the sick individual who is responsible for all this death, I prayed as I walked back to my pew with the cross on my forehead.

As I knelt down, I realized I was marked the same way the kids had been. My forehead seemed to burn. I could almost sense Jacob Dunning and Chelsea Skinner in the shadows around me. Behind my closed eyes, I could see the face of Dan Hastings, whose fate was still unknown.

Dear Lord, I prayed, *I can't let them down.*

Chapter 67

FRANCIS X. MOONEY was passing the Flat Iron Building when he shook some Dexadrine tablets into his hand. As he made it across the street into Madison Square Park, he reconsidered, dropping them into a corner trash barrel. He didn't need any speed today.

His blood felt like it was singing. In fact, everything that presented itself to his heightened senses seemed significant. The ornate architecture on the facades of the Beaux Arts buildings of lower Broadway, the scent of grease and sugar from the curbside doughnut carts, the filth-covered sidewalk beneath the soles of his shoes. None of it had ever been so vivid.

The case he carried was becoming heavier. He had to move it to his other hand every other block. Sweat from his exertion was actually making his shirt stick to his back. Still, no way would he call a taxi. His last walk, his last pilgrimage, had to be on foot.

He'd always loved the city. Walking its endlessly fascinating streets had been one of his life's greatest and simplest pleasures. The French actually coined a word for urban strollers, *flâneurs,* people who derive pleasure from observing the urban scene completely objectively and aesthetically.

But that was the problem, he thought as he walked on. He had been objective for way too long.

At the corner of 25th and Fifth, he suddenly stopped. A woman was approaching the side alley of a run-down building, carrying a white garbage bag.

"Excuse me," Francis called as he jogged over. "Miss! Miss! You there!"

She stopped.

"How dare you!" Francis said, pointing to a Diet Coke bottle clearly visible beneath the thin plastic garbage bag she was holding. "That's recycling. You're throwing out recycling!"

"What are you, the garbage police?" she said. She gave him the finger. "Get a life, you pathetic freak."

Francis thought about shooting her. His Beretta,

locked and loaded, waited at the top of the valise. Blow the smugness and the woman's ugly face clean away, kick her into the stinking alley, where she belonged. Suddenly aware of the passing pedestrians, he got a grip instead. He wouldn't let his emotions get the better of him. He had much bigger fish to fry.

But he just couldn't help himself when he stopped for the second time, on 33rd, one block south of the Empire State Building. Putting down his case, he halted before the telephone company's idling box truck on the corner.

"Excuse me!" he said to the oaf eating his breakfast behind the driver's side window. He rapped sharply with his Columbia ring on the glass right beside the jerk's face. "I said, excuse me!"

The phone guy threw open the door and leapt out onto the sidewalk. He had a shaved head and the shoulders of a defensive lineman.

"Fuck you knocking on my window for, dog?" he bellowed, spitting doughnut crumbs.

"Fuck you idling your truck for, dog?" Francis shot back. "You're violating Section twenty-four-dash-one-sixty-three of the New York City Administrative Code: 'No person shall cause or permit the engine of a motor vehicle, other than a legally authorized emergency motor vehicle, to idle for longer than three minutes while parking.' You see that poison coming out of your tailpipe there? It includes chemicals like benzene, formaldehyde, and acetaldehyde, not to mention particulate matter that can lodge deep in your lungs. It kills people, heats up the environment, too. Now shut it—"

The gaping, wide-eyed phone company man let out a kind of snort as his huge hand suddenly reached out. He snatched Francis's tie and swung him around in a full three-sixty before letting him go. Francis actually went off his feet as he slammed into a newspaper box on the corner. He skinned his chin and the palms of his hands as he went ass over tea kettle onto Fifth Avenue. Horns honked as Gotham Writers' Workshop pamphlets fluttered past his face.

Turning, Francis got a good mouthful of particulate matter–laced exhaust as the fleeing phone truck left rubber. He coughed as he pulled himself back into a sitting position on the curb.

There were pebbles embedded in his bleeding palms, a streak of something black and wet across the forearm of his tailored suit jacket. He looked down at the torn knee of his Savile Row pants. For a moment, he was back in the schoolyard again, picked on and knocked down by assholes who were bigger and older. Like it did then, the misery of feeling powerless began to bubble up.

But then, the startled fury on the phone man's face came back to him, and he was suddenly laughing. He had to stop this nonsense. He'd gotten off easy, Francis realized, considering how large the man was. He was lucky the guy hadn't killed him.

Besides, he wasn't powerless anymore, was he? he thought as he found his valise. He patted it lovingly before he lifted it and continued his pilgrimage north.

A snatch of grammar school Robert Frost came to him as he picked up his pace.

He recited to himself, *But I have promises to keep, and miles to go before I sleep.*

Chapter 68

"DADDY, DO MY ashes look okay? I told Grandpa to do a good job," my five-year-old, Chrissy, said as we sat by the window inside the crowded Starbucks at 93rd and Broadway.

We'd just dropped off her siblings at school after church. Chrissy, who was in kindergarten now, luckily didn't have to go in until noon. In our big family, one-on-one time was an extremely rare commodity. Not even a nasty killing spree would make me miss our Wednesday-morning Starbucks date.

"I don't know. Let me see," I said, reaching across the table, holding her tiny chin in my hand as I peered at her. I couldn't help but kiss her elflike nose. "They look great, Chrissy. Grandpa did fine. And they go really well with your hot chocolate mustache."

As she went back to her drink, I looked at the long line by the pastry case. Waiting for their morning fix of Seattle's main export were nannies with infants, tired-looking construction workers, and tired-looking men and women dressed in business clothes. Maybe ten percent of them, along with one of the baristas, had ashes.

I wondered with a cold chill if it was in the killer's mind to shoot people who had ashes today. That he was going to do *something* was a given. Every indication was that today was the day. The only questions left were where and how.

I rubbed my eyes before I lifted my coffee and took a large gulp. My blood caffeine level had hit record highs in the past couple of sleepless days, but it couldn't be helped. After last night's end-of-day task force meeting, I'd spent much of the night Googling everything I could on Ash Wednesday.

Ash Wednesday was one of the most solemn days in the Catholic liturgical year. It was a day for contemplating one's transgressions.

But whose transgressions was the killer trying to point out with the slayings? The dead kids'? Society's? His own?

I caught my ash-streaked, mournful reflection in the plate glass.

Well, I was certainly stewing in my own lapses this morning, I thought, looking away. For not already putting an end to this horrible case.

As Chrissy played peekaboo with a neighboring toddler in a stroller, I checked my cell phone for the millionth time to see if I had missed any messages. I winced when only my Yankees-logo wallpaper appeared again. Emily had put an incredible rush on the print, but there was still no word.

I spun my phone on the chessboard tabletop as I looked out the window down Broadway. I could feel the moments slipping away from me, and there was nothing I could do.

Where and how? I thought. *Where and how?*

Chapter 69

MY CASE-DISTRACTED MIND still hadn't come a hundred percent back online as I stepped with Chrissy into my apartment ten minutes later. Otherwise, I would have checked my caller ID before I snapped open my phone.

"What's the story?" I yelled into it.

"What story?" my grandfather Seamus said. "Actually, who cares? Did you tell her yet?"

"Tell who what?"

"Mary Catherine, ya eedjit! See, I knew you'd forget. And with MC in such a riled knot of late. Does the song 'Happy Birthday' ring a bell, Detective?"

"Holy sh— . . . ugar," I said. "No. I forgot."

Eedjit was right! I thought. I'd blown this one

big-time. I could at least have brought her back a muffin or something. What would Mary Catherine throw out of mine next? I wondered. I needed to address the situation, and pronto. I heard the tea kettle start to boil in the kitchen. Maybe I still had a shot.

"I'm all over it, Father," I said, hanging up.

Mary was taking a mug down from the cabinet just inside the kitchen door.

"Mary. There you are," I said, surprising her with a hug.

"Happy birthday!" I said as merrily as I could and went to plant a kiss on her cheek.

But as it turned out, I was the one who got the surprise present.

Mary Catherine turned her head, and our lips locked. At first, I pulled back as if I'd been Tasered, but then, before I knew it, my hand found the back of her neck and we were, well, *making out* would be the exact expression.

Mary's unheeded mug slid off the counter and shattered.

I guess you could call it pretty hot-and-heavy making out.

"Mary Catherine!" Chrissy called a second later just outside the kitchen door.

Mary almost broke my nose as she ripped herself

away from me. Her face was at least twenty shades redder than her strawberry-blond hair. My face felt like it was on fire. I couldn't seem to close my mouth.

"Goddamn you, Mike," she said before she fled out the doorway. Was she crying? Why was she crying? I was having trouble enough breathing. I heard the hall bathroom door slam a second later.

I was still standing there, brain-locked and blinking, when Chrissy came in. "Where's MC?" she said.

"I'm not sure. I broke a mug, Chrissy. Could you get me the dustpan?"

Chapter 70

I WAS DOWN on my hands and knees, dazed and sweeping up, when my cell rattled.

"Hey, Mike," Agent Parker said. "Get down here. I have news. I'm right outside your building."

"Thank God," I said, dumping the last of the shards into the garbage. "I mean, on my way!"

I quickly hollered, "I'm off to work, 'bye, Mary," as I passed the still-closed bathroom door.

Was that the right thing to do? I wasn't sure. I'd never made out with my kids' nanny before.

I wiped the lip gloss off my chin in the elevator mirror on the way down to the street. Still tasting it, I pondered what the heck had just happened and how I felt about it.

Like I needed something else on my plate at this juncture.

"Goddamn you, Mike."

Chapter 71

I CLIMBED INTO Emily's double-parked Crown Vic. She was wearing a new white silk blouse and sleek beige skirt suit. With the case dragging on, she must have done some shopping, I realized.

Was it me, or was the blouse showing some pretty nice cleavage? I wiped my eyes. What the hell was happening to me?

"Feeling okay there, Mike?"

"Never better," I said, smiling. "What's up?"

Emily handed me a folder.

"We finally got the toxicology report back on the ashes found on the first victim, Jacob Dunning. Are you familiar with X-ray fluorescence spectroscopy?"

"Had one six months ago," I said, nodding. "Doctor said I'm as clean as a whistle."

"Listen closely, wiseass," Emily said, ignoring my acerbic wit. "Basically, individual elements reflect X-ray light in different patterns. They ran the ashes through the machine, and it turns out most of it is regular cigarette tobacco. The twist is that they found traces of some very interesting substances as well that came from the killer's sweat."

"Like what kind of substances?" I said.

Emily lifted a clipboard.

"Several amphetamines and a drug called . . . Iressa. It's a chemotherapy drug for lung cancer."

I rubbed my face as I nodded.

"Hey, good work," I said. "I'll get Schultz to contact Sloan-Kettering and the other cancer centers and check out their patients. It's starting to make a little more sense now in terms of motive. If this guy is terminal, maybe he made out some psycho bucket list. Maybe this is his way of going out with a bang."

"Funny you should say *bang*," Emily said, pointing to a name on the fax sheet. "Because the drugs aren't the worst of it. There was evidence of something called pentaerythritol. It's found in plastic explosives, Mike."

Chapter 72

KIDNAPPING, CHILD MURDERS, and now plastic explosives? This nightmare case kept getting worse and worse. I unsuccessfully tried to wake myself out of it as Emily answered her encrypted cell phone.

"Hold on, Tom," she said into it. "Let me put you on speaker."

"We got the print back, Em," FBI lab chief Tom Warriner said a moment later. "You're not going to believe this. It's a hit, but one that's coded to COINTELPRO."

"Cointelpro?" I said.

"The FBI's counterintelligence program," Emily said.

"The section attached to this was run out of the New York office," Warriner continued. "The Domestic Terrorism Squad from the sixties. The code name attached is Shadowbox."

"In Intelligence Squads, when the identity of a person is classified, they designate code names," Emily explained with a roll of her eyes. "Like the CIA, the FBI spook division loves codes and passwords. James Bond, eat your heart out."

She aimed her voice at her phone.

"So, what do you think, Tom? Our guy, this Shadowbox, was probably a confidential informant on a domestic terrorist group?"

Terrorism? I was still trying to absorb the plastic explosives angle.

"Most likely," the FBI lab chief said.

"So, how do we get a name to match the code name?" I asked.

"I've tried twice to crack the old databases, but some COINTELPRO records seem to be missing," Warriner said.

Emily snorted.

"I'll bet. Into the ol' memory hole you go. What the hell are we going to do? How do we get around that?"

"I've been asking around, and the best lead I can tell

you is that you guys should go see John Browning," Warriner said. "He's the former agent who ran the group out of the New York office from 'sixty-eight to 'seventy-four. I tried to call him, but there's no answer at his house up in Yonkers. I worked with Browning on a few things when I was a rookie tech. Sarcastic pain in the ass, but a mind like a steel trap. If he can't tell you who Shadowbox is, no one can."

Chapter 73

THE CROWN VIC'S V8 screamed like it meant it as we zigzagged north up the crowded Saw Mill River Parkway. Danica Patrick had nothing on Emily Parker, I thought as I white-knuckled the door handle.

Browning lived on a cul-de-sac near the Dunwoodie golf course. There was a U-Haul truck in his driveway. *Please don't be moved out,* I prayed as we came to a hard stop behind it.

A wiry, clean-cut sixty- or maybe seventy-something-year-old in a St. John's University sweatshirt came out of the garage, carrying a box of model trains. I noticed he'd gotten his ashes today as well.

"Help you?" he said, his intelligent blue eyes shifting quickly from me to Emily.

"We hope so," Emily said, showing him her tin. "Tom Warriner sent us. It's about CO—"

He lifted a pausing finger as a woman came out of the house across the street, carrying a tray of plants.

"It's about your, um, previous line of work," Emily finished in a lower voice.

"I see," he said. "Come on in, then, I guess," he said, waving us toward the open garage door.

"Finally heading to Florida," he said after he closed the garage door behind him. "Just sold to a rent refugee. Yuppie couple from Manhattan. Said they wanted their Yorkies to have some room to stretch out. I managed to raise four daughters here, so maybe it'll work out for them."

"We need your help, John," Emily said quickly. "We need to cut through a mountain of red tape, and we're running out of time. In 'sixty-nine, you ran a CI named Shadowbox. His print just came up in the system. We think he has something to do with these kid killings that are going on in the city."

"I see," he said, tapping a finger to his cheek.

"If you want, you could call Tom to confirm my ID," Emily said.

"You kidding me?" Browning said, rolling his eyes at me. "I knew you were Government before your Mary Janes hit my driveway. Shadowbox's name was Mooney. Francis Xavier Mooney. Pale college kid. Wore glasses. Smart, smart kid from a blue-collar family in Inwood. He went to Columbia but got in with some seriously radical people. After he got busted for dope, he advised us on a case we were building on an offshoot of the Weathermen terrorist group."

"Shit," I said. "There's that *T* word again."

Browning nodded.

"One night he calls me late and tells me about a bomb-making factory his boys got going in an apartment in the Village. Said his buddies were about to blow up Grand Central Terminal. We go to raid the place and *baboom!* One of the jackasses running for the back window knocked over something he shouldn't have and the place went up. Took down half the building. Four of them died. Mooney was torn up over it. Like he blamed himself. We took him out of the program after that. Last I heard of him."

"When was this?"

"Oh...," the retired agent said, looking up at his garage ceiling. "It was in nineteen seventy. What's that? Almost forty years ago?"

His expression changed. He actually looked a little ruffled for a moment.

"It was Ash Wednesday nineteen seventy. We

called it the Ash Wednesday bombing. Terrorists and anniversaries. Not good."

I beat Emily by half a thumb press of my cell phone.

"Get on this," I told Schultz as he picked up at the task force. "The suspect's name is Francis Xavier Mooney. Address most likely in Manhattan. He might have explosives. Tell them to beef up security at Grand Central. It may be a potential target. Call me back the second you have this guy's address."

"How many he kill?" Browning said as we waited for his rattling garage door to go back up.

"Two, maybe three kids," I said.

He shook his head.

"Not surprised. Frigging nut case. Even after we hosed his friends from the rubble, he was going on about that freegan, tree-hugging crap. Be careful. Mooney's an idealist. One thing I learned during my illustrious career is that they're always the ones you have to watch the closest."

Chapter 74

THE SKIES OPENED up as we tore back to the highway from the former FBI agent's house. The thump of the speeding wipers almost managed to keep time with my racing heart. My adrenaline was jacked. Closing in on Mooney was better than drinking a case of Red Bull.

My cell rang as we hydroplaned onto the parkway entrance.

"Mike," Chief Fleming said. "We just got the ten-seven on Mooney. He lives in Chelsea. Four-four-eight West Twenty-fifth. That's between Ninth and Tenth about three blocks from the Fashion Institute of Technology."

"Finally!" I screamed. I repeated the address to

Emily. After all the dead ends and frustration, for the first time in the case, we were on the hunt.

"Since Mooney might still have a hold of Dan Hastings," my boss continued, "the ADIC from the New York FBI office just authorized the Hostage Rescue Team to do the assault. They're en route to Chelsea right now along with our bomb guys.

"We're still working on the no-knock warrant. Harry Dobbins, chief of the DA's Homicide Division, wrote it up himself and is going to call me from Centre Street the second he can find a judge to sign it. Where are you?"

"About thirty minutes out," I said. "Where'd you get Mooney's address? From a criminal record?"

"No, get this," the chief said. "His name popped up in the city social workers registration database. I just got off the phone with them. He's part-time, and his record says that he's an attorney with Ericsson, Weymouth and Roth, on Lexington. I've heard of them. A top-flight corporate firm. ESU's on its way over there."

"Do you have their number?" I said.

As I dialed the firm, I spotted the agonizingly distant Manhattan skyline through a break of parkway trees. Goddammit. We needed to be there yesterday.

Had Mooney struck yet? Would he hit his office? Were we too late?

"Ericsson, Weymouth and Roth. May I put you on hold?" said a pleasant female voice.

"Hell, no!" I yelled. "This is Detective Mike Bennett of the NYPD. This is extremely urgent. I need to know if Francis X. Mooney came to work today."

"Mr. Mooney? He's one of our senior partners. I can patch you through to his voice mail," the voice said.

"Listen to me!" I screamed. "We have reason to believe *Mr.* Mooney is armed and extremely dangerous, suicidal, and homicidal. Has he come in? Yes or no?"

"Oh, my God!" the woman said. "I'm not sure."

"Check now!" I yelled.

The phone thumped down.

"I just spoke to his secretary," the receptionist said. "He's not here. The office manager is right here, though."

"This is Ted Provencal," said a man a moment later.

"Mike Bennett from the NYPD. We have reason to believe that your coworker Francis Mooney is responsible for the rash of recent teenage killings."

I heard the man breathing heavily. He seemed stunned.

"Francis?" he said. "Francis?!"

"I know it's a shock. But I need as much information about him as I can gather. Where is he right now?"

"I don't know. He has no meetings scheduled. Francis has been in and out recently. Ever since he was diagnosed with lung cancer, we rolled his casework back. He's been on flex time."

So that explained the drug, I thought.

"Mooney has cancer?" I said.

"Stage four, non-small-cell," the man said. "He found out three months ago. Too far gone to even do surgery, the poor guy. He was a two-pack-a-day man. We begged him to quit. Offered him incentives. It seemed so stupid for such a brilliant man."

"He's smart? How smart?"

"Without question one of the smartest men I've ever known. And meticulous? If he ever missed a detail in a contract or a will, I never heard about it. He was the head of our Estates and Trusts division. One of the most popular people in the whole firm, too, with both colleagues and clients. He even ran our pro bono department. I mean, are you a hundred percent sure he's involved? That horrible thing from the paper? Those kids who were shot? It's truly unbelievable. Are you sure?"

"Believe it," I hollered at him. "Police are on their way. Lock down your office, and tell your security chief to keep Mooney out of the building at all costs. He's armed, and we think he might have explosives."

Chapter 75

WE WERE SCREECHING off the West Side Highway at 23rd in Chelsea when Emily received a call on her Fed phone. We were directed to an ugly beige-brick high-rise around the corner from Eighth Avenue and 25th Street.

As we swerved down into its underground garage, a large, dirty white box truck flashed its lights at us. Emily stopped behind the truck's graffiti-covered back gate.

The gate rolled up, revealing a spotless interior filled with racks of computer servers and screens. It seemed like every inch of the walls was layered in cables for the very complicated-looking electronics equipment. What was most surprising by far, though, were the half dozen men dressed in tactical black, securing submachine guns on a bench along both walls. They completely ignored us as they busily tightened the snaps and clips on their various weapons and gear.

"HRT's Mobile Tactical Operations Center," Emily explained as we climbed in. "State-of-the-art surveillance setup and command center rolled into one. There's fiber-optic cameras and boom microphones, as well as audio and visual com links to all the forward sniper observers."

"Welcome to your Homeland Security dollars hard at work," a handsome young Asian agent said as he flipped up his ballistic goggles and gave Emily a quick fist tap.

"Mike, meet Tom Chow. He's head of HRT two," Emily said.

Chow pointed to a computer screen showing a two-story brick town house.

"Thar she blows," he said. "We've been here about half an hour, and there's been no movement in or out. We can't confirm if he's inside."

From beside the computer, Chow lifted up some photographs of Mooney's building taken from various overhead angles.

"We figure we have two breach points, the roof and the front door," he said, pointing them out. "See this other taller building to the east alongside? That's a warehouse. We already have a team up there ready to fast-rope down to Mooney's roof deck and gain entry. Sniper observers across the street will cover the windows so the rest of us, the breach team, can blow the front door. EMS is around on Tenth, ready to come in once we locate the kid."

Chow turned as an oversized NYPD van pulled in behind our car. A black Labrador wagged its tail on the front seat between two cops wearing bulky gray bomb-proof suits.

"Hey, now," Chow said. "Even the Bomb Squad is here. Time to get this party started."

Chow pulled a ringing cell phone from his fatigues a moment later. He listened briefly. He was smiling as he shut it. He lowered his goggles and pounded on the tinted Plexiglas that separated the back of the assault truck from its cab.

"That's the green light, people. We got it. Roll this sister."

Emily and I strapped on borrowed vests as the truck's back gate rolled down. My stomach rolled, too, as the truck suddenly lurched forward up the ramp.

A split second later, the truck came to a whiplash-inducing stop. Its back door went up like a snapped shade, and the FBI commandos sprinted out onto the street toward the town house. Faster than they could ring the doorbell, a charge was placed by the knob, and Mooney's door blew back into the house with a low thump.

Two men in black rappelled off the building beside the town house as the commandos on the street rushed into it behind their Heckler and Koch MP5s.

In a chaos of radio chatter and shouts, I followed them over the sidewalk with my Glock drawn. Emily was right on my heels with a Remington shotgun.

"Please be home, fucker," she said at my back as we ran.

"Yes, fucker," I agreed. "Please, pretty please, be home."

Chapter 76

AS THE DOOR to his town house was being blown into tiny pieces, Francis X. Mooney stopped on the corner of Park Avenue sixty blocks to the northeast and set down his bag.

He turned toward the four-story Gothic school building that took up most of the north side of 85th Street between Park and Lexington. It was St. Edward's Academy, the elite private school he had attended from seventh grade through senior year.

He was filthy from his scuffle, wet from the rain, and completely exhausted from the walk, but he'd made it, hadn't he?

He'd come back full circle to the place where it had all begun.

He stood for a second, remembering his first day here. He'd stood in this same spot, sick and frozen, with the scholarship-kid certainty that his clothes, his face, and every other inch of his being wouldn't be up to snuff.

He quickly removed the Beretta from the valise and tucked it into the waistband of his trousers and smoothed his jacket over it.

The butterflies never changed, he thought, finally hefting his case with a swallow of his dry throat.

Just the reasons.

I can't do this, he thought.

I must do this, he thought.

"Francis? Francis, is that you?"

Francis turned. A tall, lean black man about his age was stopped beside him, smiling. He wore a St. Edward's ball cap and held a takeout bag.

"Do I know you?" Francis said.

"I hope so. It's me, Jerry Webb. We were on varsity together, class of 'sixty-five. It's actually Coach Webb now. I was in finance for a while, but then I came back to good old St. Ed's to teach them how to play a little ball. Can you imagine? I can't sometimes, especially when I get my paycheck."

"Oh, my God. Jerry. Yes," Francis said, recovering. He found himself smiling genuinely as he shook the tall man's hand. They actually had been teammates. If you could really call them that. Webb had been their all-city starting power forward, while Francis had had to practically kill himself every practice just for the privilege of riding the bench.

"It's been—," Francis began.

"Too long," Coach Webb said with a wink. "Ol' Francis X. Blast from the past. I knew that was you. Not too old yet to pick an old teammate out of a crowd. Can you still drive to your left like a banshee, ma man?"

Francis's smile immediately dissipated. He'd never been able to go to his left. It was the first string's running joke. Had Webb been one of the ones in that incident at summer practice? Francis went over the still-raw forty-year-old memory. He nodded to himself. Indeed he had.

"What brings you around?" the still-cocky bastard wanted to know as he gave Francis the once-over. "You're looking a little ruffled."

How polite of you to notice, Francis thought.

"I had an appointment with a law client around the corner. First, I slipped getting out of my taxi, then I got caught in the rain, and then the guy bailed on me," Francis lied. "Long story short, not my day. I thought, since I was in the neighborhood, I might stick my head in the door to check on the application of one of my friends' kids."

"Oh, I know how that goes," Coach Webb said. "One tradition about St. Ed's that remains unchanged. It never seems to get any easier to get into, does it? Let's walk in together."

The flat-topped middle-aged guard behind the arched glass doors immediately buzzed them in when he spotted the coach. Francis swallowed again as he stepped inside. This was the hard part coming up. He hadn't had time to do reconnaissance, and he wasn't sure if his flimsy excuse would hold water.

"He's with me, Tommy," Coach Webb said, signing them both into the security register. "This here's Francis X., a valued alum. He's got very important business at Admissions. I'll walk him there myself."

"No problem, Coach," the guard said with a thumbs-up.

Francis wiped his brow as they walked down the locker-lined hallway. He glanced into classrooms as they passed. He started to panic. What the hell? They were all empty.

"Where is everybody?" he said as casually as he could.

"Sports pep rally in the auditorium. Baseball went

to the Staties last season. Now, if only I could get my guys there."

A pep rally. Would that complicate things? Probably. No time to do anything about it. He'd just have to improvise somehow.

Coach Webb patted Francis on the shoulder as they stopped before a door marked ADMISSIONS.

"Come visit me anytime, Francis. To jaw or maybe go a little one-on-one. See if that left of yours is still in operating order. Great seeing you, ma man."

"You, too, Jerry. Thanks for everything," Francis said with a grin.

Thanks for helping me set in motion the blackest day in St. Edward's history, you conceited jock moron, he thought as he watched him walk away.

Chapter 77

IT TOOK HIM thirty seconds to backtrack down the hall to the main office. An old platinum-haired woman in a Harris tweed skirt suit was typing by herself behind the counter. A soft Muzak version of "I Left My Heart in San Francisco" was coming from the radio beside her keyboard.

"Hello. May I help you?" the woman said in a highly polished voice. She was smiling as she turned, an attractive, bright-eyed woman in her early seventies. She lowered her bifocals.

Francis suddenly felt numb. It was one thing to do someone in a private place, to do someone in the dark, in secret. This was different, he realized. Beads of sweat stood on his hot forehead. Out here, under the blazing fluorescents with the Muzak playing, was very goddamned different.

Now! a voice in his head chided him.

Francis kicked the door shut behind him and breathed in loudly.

The woman was starting to stand when he leapt over the counter and grabbed her by her scratchy lapel. He fumbled the sheet from his pocket. On the printed sheet were photographs of two St. Edward's students, along with their names. He didn't know who was shaking more, her or him.

"D-di-did these children come to school today?" he stammered.

"What? Let go of me this instant! You can't do this! Who are you?"

"Listen to me!" Francis yelled. He took the silenced Beretta from his waistband and put it to her head.

"Did these children come to school today?" he said again.

The old woman started to cry when she saw the gun.

"Please!" she shrieked as she tried to pull away. She'd closed her eyes and was really blubbering now. "No, please. Why do you want those students? Don't hurt me! What are you doing?"

Damn it, Francis thought, shaking her. This wasn't how it was supposed to go.

He turned at a soft rushing noise behind him. It was the door. Francis saw Coach Webb standing there, wide-eyed.

"What in the name of Holy God are you doing?" the coach said.

Francis let go of the woman. His mouth dropped open as he met his old teammate's eyes. Caught. Holy shit. Caught.

His body and mind seemed to arrest simultaneously. He felt like his breath had been knocked out of him. The gun suddenly felt unbelievably heavy in his hand.

It was over. He was too weak. He knew it. He shouldn't even be up on his feet at this point. Where was he now? Stage four? Deep stage four. He was a very sick man, a weak, dying old man. He should be in a hospital bed over at Sloan-Kettering.

"Put it down, Francis," Coach Webb said. "Now, man."

Can you still drive to your left like a banshee, ma man? Francis heard him say again. A quick memory flashed through Francis's mind. Webb in the gym bathroom doorway, howling as he held the elastic of Francis's torn tighty whiteys above his head.

He grabbed on to the pulse of hurt and rage that throbbed through him. It was like a second wind. Francis retightened his grip on the pistol. His resolve. He raised the gun.

"How about instead you get in here and close that fucking door, *ma man,*" he said. The coach looked like he was about to bolt down the hall, but then he shot a look over at Ms. Typing-to-the-Oldies and suddenly obeyed.

Webb was turning back from closing the door when Francis pulled the trigger. The bullet hit him right in his smug power-forward-all-city face. He fell back comically fast, as if he'd slipped on a banana peel. *Swoosh!* Nothing but net! Francis thought with a chuckle. What did they say at Knicks games again? *Whoomp! There it is!*

Francis felt amazingly focused as he turned back to the woman. It was as if someone had turned up the dimmer switch of his energy as far as it would go.

"Did those children come to school today?" he said again clearly and confidently, his best courtroom voice. He knocked her glasses away and placed the warm gun barrel on one of her squinted-shut eyelids.

"Yes," she said.

The woman was weeping silently. Francis suddenly noticed that he was as well.

So much blood and still more to come, he thought. He nodded. It was worth it and then some.

"It was brave of you to try to protect the kids," Francis whispered lovingly in the old lady's ear. "But a higher purpose is waiting for them. That's why I'm here. To deliver unto them the very highest purpose of all."

Chapter 78

COUGHING IN THE flash-bang grenade smoke, I found a window in Mooney's kitchen and threw it open.

"Goddang!" Emily rebel-yelled as she laid her pump shotgun on the granite kitchen island. "We missed his ass."

"Damn it," I said with disgust.

I loosened one of the Velcro straps on the heavy body armor and sat down next to her. Hostage Rescue had scoured every room on both floors, and there was nothing. No one was home. No Mooney. And even worse, no Dan Hastings.

After a quick call to my boss, I learned that Mooney still hadn't shown up to work. Which was good in a way, since he just might be looking to kill everyone there. But if not at work, then where was he?

"Where should we toss first?" I said.

"Office," she said.

We went up to the second floor and pooched through his office. And by *pooched,* I mean we tore it apart. In filing cabinets, we found trusts and estates folders, take-home work from his job probably. One of the walls was covered with photos of Francis at high-profile charity events. There were quite a few framed *Vanity Fair* and *Avenue* magazine pages. A business card in a side drawer said Mooney was something called a Philanthropy Consultant. To high-net-worth individuals, no doubt, by the gala events he was often photographed at.

One of the commandos called to us excitedly from downstairs.

"I think I found something, Em," Chow said as we arrived in the basement. He pointed his gun-barrel-mounted flashlight at an open door. I reached in and flicked on the light switch.

I stood there, blinking, but not at the light. Against cement walls stood stack upon stack of newspapers and books. They were six feet high in some places. It looked like a pretty eclectic collection. There was a whole section of anti-Bush nonfiction. Well-thumbed tomes of Spinoza. A book called *Quantum Geometry of Bosonic Strings* sat on top of an autobiography of Martin Luther King, Jr. I spotted some French-language Rousseau and Alexis de Tocqueville volumes that had margin notes handwritten in French. There were many books by Jean-Paul Sartre and the modern French philosopher Michel Foucault.

"This guy might be a killer and a kook," Emily said, "but at least he's a well-read one."

In a metal filing cabinet drawer we found a laptop. Emily pulled on surgical gloves before she turned it on. The laptop's whole screen was filled with numbered Word documents.

Emily clicked on a random one. It was random, all right.

" 'They must be shown,' " she read. " 'Communication is futile. Like Malcolm X, I, too, am branded with the philosophy of any-means-necessary. I, too, am a free-willed, informed human being who has gifts that transcend the ordinary. I, too, have responsibilities that transcend the ordinary. I, too, have—' "

" 'A mental disease that transcends the ordinary,' " I finished for her.

"It goes on and on," Emily said, scrolling with the mouse. "Oh, my God, it's five hundred pages. There must be a hundred of these documents. It'll take months to dredge through this nonsense."

That's when we heard the barking.

It was the bomb dog. He was at the top of the basement stairs, barking down at us, going absolutely crazy.

"I don't think he needs to be walked," Chow yelled. "Clear it! Now! Everybody out!"

He didn't have to tell us twice. We were across the cordoned-off street on the safe side of the SWAT truck when the bomb guys came out ten minutes later. Each of them was holding a cardboard box.

The older, mustached bomb tech waved me over to the back of his van. I swallowed. I didn't think he was inviting me to tailgate with him.

"Better you than me, Mike," Emily said, sticking her fingers in her ears.

"Found it in the crawl space next to the basement office," the bomb cop said as I approached. I gingerly looked into the box he was holding. Inside was a stack of long white blocks that looked like they were made of Crisco.

"Relax. It's C-four," the veteran cop said with a dismissive wave. "Well, actually, I'm pretty sure it's PE-four, the very similar British version of the plastic explosive. It's totally stable. You could play stickball with it. Hell, you could light it on fire and nothing would happen. Nothing happens unless you wire it to..."

He paused while he showed me the other box, which contained a reel of what looked like thick green clothesline.

“A detonator. This one here is called Cordtex. It looks like rope, acts like rope, but it has an explosive core that makes it one long mother of a blasting cap. You can fell a tree with six feet of it. Or a building if you connect it with enough of the PE-four from box number one.”

The bomb cop stroked his mustache and sighed in a way that raised the hair on the back of my neck.

“What?” I said.

“The problem is the box,” he said.

“The box?” I said.

“The PE-four came in a twenty-five-pound box. There’s only six or seven pounds here. Also, I’d say about half the reel of det cord is missing.”

I didn’t have a mustache, so I rubbed my temples instead as I turned and took in the 360-degree city vista of buildings and buses and pedestrians. Targets as far as the eye could see. Mooney could be anywhere at all.

“Shit,” I said.

“You said it,” the bomb cop said.

Chapter 79

FRANCIS ADJUSTED THE St. Edward's ball cap that he had taken from the dead coach as he walked quickly through the school's empty corridors. He smiled as he passed his old chem lab. How the rest of them had hated him for always wrecking the curve with his near-perfect scores.

He opened a door into the empty lower school's practice gym. It still smelled like sweat and Bengay. He gazed at the thick patina of paint on the walls, the battered gates on the tall windows. How many layups had he made across its parquet? How many laps around the dusty loft track above? Passing across, he unscrewed the silencer from the Beretta and hook-shot it at the hoop from the top of the key. It fell short by at least three feet.

"Air ball. What else is new?" he grumbled, pocketing the pistol.

The roar of the crowd hit him like a smack as he came through a door into the cavernous upper-school gym. The stands were filled with the all-boy student body. In their blazers and khakis, they looked somewhat similar to his class, though their long hair and loose ties would have earned them a detention in his oppressive day. There were a lot more brown faces now, though, so at least some progress had been made.

"Let's go, St. Ed's!" the headmaster was chanting through a bullhorn. "Here we go, St. Ed's!" Beside him, kids with baseball jerseys over their ties were pumping their fists and waving their arms upward for more noise.

The sound reminded him of the all-city semifinal. The heat and cheers and the smash of the ball against the parquet. He hadn't played a minute in it, despite what the coach had promised. Webb had won it for them at the buzzer. He'd left as they were raising that shit heel on their shoulders. He'd certainly received a terrific education at St. Edward's, though. It was here where he first learned how entirely shitty humanity could be.

People were staring at him as he came along the stands.

He pointed at his hat and waved at them vigorously.

"Here we go, St. Ed's!" he yelled along with the crowd as he approached the stage.

The headmaster was jumping up and down, letting off an air horn, when Francis jumped on the stage beside him. His face scrunched in surprise as Mooney put the gun to his temple.

"I am a good person," Francis said to him as he ripped the bullhorn from his hands.

Chapter 80

BRANDISHING THE UGLY black pistol high above his head, Mooney looked out at the students. The team members had splayed themselves flat alongside the padded wall to the gym's rear. In the stands directly beneath the newly hung baseball championship banner, a male teacher was leaning to the side, selflessly trying to shield as many students as he could.

Mooney took a measured breath, fighting down his pounding pulse. He had their rapt attention now. The happy shouts of the six-hundred-strong student body cut off suddenly as if Mooney had pressed a Mute button.

In the sudden hush, the bald headmaster's

terrified breath beside him sounded like he was doing Lamaze. Mooney laid the four-inch barrel of the Beretta against his hairless forehead as he raised the bullhorn.

"Everybody, stay in your seats," Mooney called out. "Anyone who tries to run will be shot dead. I don't want to cut your young lives short, but I will. Something must be done. This is it. I'm doing it."

Warm sweat poured freely down Francis's face. All that remained of the ashes he had gotten that morning was a faint streak.

Some of the students in the stands seemed oddly fascinated, perhaps in shock. Several young men were fumbling two-handed with their cell phones, texting for help, no doubt. He spotted one none-too-subtle ugly blond kid at the top of the bleachers pointing his camera phone toward the stage. The situation was probably already streaming onto the Internet.

Yes. Let it go out over YouTube, he thought. Let it go out everywhere around the globe. That's what was needed here. What better impact than something happening real time to shout his message into the deaf ears of the world?

Francis saw that some kids were crying. Tears started to stream unheeded down his own face.

"You were supposed to be the future leaders of this

country," he called to them. "I know this because I attended this prestigious academy myself. Now I've come to give you the ultimate test of your worthiness, the ultimate test of your character."

The megaphone squawked grating feedback as Francis toggled its trigger.

"Listen to me!" he cried. "Question one: While you were playing the Metal Gear and Sniper Elite video games you received at Christmas, how many real-war casualties were there in Iraq and Afghanistan? In Darfur?"

Chapter 81

IT WAS FULL-OUT bedlam on 25th Street in front of Mooney's doorless town house. The bomb techs and black-clad Hostage Rescue Team agents were now joined by another thirty or so Manhattan Task Force uniforms, who had come to secure the crime scene.

Positioned center stage on the sidewalk behind the tape, Emily and I paced like expectant parents, calling everyone and anyone we could think of to track down Mooney.

We'd sent Schultz with a team to Inwood to Mooney's mother's apartment. Ramirez was over at his law firm, trying to shake some new leads loose, but so far he had come up with diddly.

Every few seconds, streaks of bubbling blue-and-red light from speeding PD radio cars would blow past on Ninth, their sirens *whoop-whoop*ing.

"The commissioner has put on the department's entire day shift and activated the NYPD Anti-Terror Task Force Hercules team," my boss, Carol Fleming, told me. "Cars and personnel are being deployed to Times Square, Rockefeller Center, all the major population clusters in the city."

I blew out a frustrated breath. They really had their work cut out for them, considering that Manhattan was actually one large population cluster.

"The commissioner also wants to know yesterday how the hell Mooney got his hands on British military plastic explosive," I was told.

"I'll be sure to ask him after I read him his rights," I told my boss before I hung up.

"Yeah, his last rites," mumbled Emily, who seemed even more pissed than me.

I glanced at her and came close to chuckling. I remembered way back, three days before, when Parker was a rube Fibbie. Now she was starting to sound like me.

"New York–style bitterness and sarcasm," I said. "You're starting to impress me, Agent Parker."

Both ends of the narrow cross street in the heart of

Chelsea were cordoned off now, but of course, more and more people kept arriving by the minute to get a gander. It looked like a street fair near the barricaded bodega on the corner of Ninth. *Rent* cast member look-alikes were hanging out their windows across the street, standing on their fire escapes with binoculars, gaping down from the roofs. Hadn't they heard about the possibility of explosives? Guess not.

I hadn't even had time to put my phone away when my boss called me back.

"Mike, this is—oh, God—something new. Get a Wi-Fi connection. Go to a website called Twitpic. There's an almost-live podcast called *School Takeover*."

"*School what?!*" I yelled.

Without hanging up, I raced Emily into the back of the FBI truck and found a laptop. I clicked on Internet Explorer and brought up the website.

I opened up the link.

"Tell me that's a hoax," Emily pleaded as she looked over my shoulder.

It wasn't. My breath left me.

It was a still photo of Mooney. He was standing on a gym stage, holding a megaphone in one hand and a gun in the other. The gun was pressed to the head of another man—a teacher?—in a suit. In front of him were hundreds of male high school students wearing private school blazers.

Staring at the man and the terrified children in front of him, I felt an almost out-of-body anger. This was it. Mooney's last stand. I noticed a large bag beside him. The bomb tech told me that a pound of the PE-4 could blow up a truck. I didn't even want to think about what nineteen pounds of it could do to all those kids.

"Came in five minutes ago. It's real," my boss said.

"What school is it?" I cried.

"We've had three calls into nine-one-one in the past ten minutes from mothers whose kids go to St. Edward's Academy on the Upper East Side. Kids have been texting that a man with a gun just came into their school gym during a pep rally."

My head dropped until it was practically between my knees. Now Mooney had taken over a school full of children. This was our absolute worst nightmare come true.

"What school?" Emily said.

She jumped back as I punched the side of the truck.

"St. Edwards. It's an all-boys private prep school off Park Avenue. The richest schoolkids in the city."

"We have radio cars arriving on scene right now," my boss said. "Get up there!"

Chapter 82

IT WAS ONE long yellow blur of taxis outside the windshield as we zipped up Park Avenue. Uniformed doormen and pedestrians stood frozen under the sidewalk awnings, staring after us fearfully. I don't know which was louder, our siren or the static from the FBI radio as its frequency was flooded with city-wide emergency calls.

We skidded to a stop by the armada of blacked-out Chevy Suburbans that had taken up position across East 81st Street.

The SUVs belonged to the NYPD's intimidating Anti-Terror Hercules Squad. The Special Forces–like team of cops was positioned behind mailboxes and parked cars, aiming their M4 assault rifles at an imposing Gothic-style school building halfway down the block.

A Bentley Continental shrieked to a stop beside us. A sleek silver-haired man in pinstripes and silk suspenders jumped out, leaving the door open. A uniformed cop stiff-armed him as he tried to push over an NYPD sawhorse.

"Let me go. My son's a St. Edward's student. He's in there!" he yelled, tussling with the officer.

I noticed that a rail-thin woman in Jackie O shades was already at the opposite corner, standing beside a Range Rover Westminster with a uniformed chauffeur. A diamond-encrusted hand covered her mouth.

"Please," she said with a Russian accent to the closest officer. "His name is Terrence Osipov. Please, where is he? He's in the seventh grade."

"How exclusive is this school again?" Emily said, doing a double-take at the woman's gems.

"You kidding me?" I said. "Kindergarten at St. Edward's is thirty K according to the latest *New York* magazine. Not only is it practically as expensive as Harvard, it's harder to get into."

I found a youthful black precinct captain directing cops underneath an apartment house awning on the north side of the street.

"We spoke to the security guard," the young chief said. "He said the kook came in about half an hour ago to go to the Admissions office. Apparently he's got a gun, and he's locked himself inside the gym with the students. There was some kind of pep rally going on. The entire school is in there."

"First thing we need to do is evacuate the block," Tim Curtin, the bomb tech, said, arriving behind me. "He sets off that plastic in the right place, the gas lines could go."

HRT chief Tom Chow looked at the building through binoculars as the thump of a just-arriving NYPD Bell chopper appeared in the slot of sky above the street's limestone co-ops.

"We need to do this textbook," he said. "Block off all routes of escape. Take up shooting positions on the surrounding buildings. Approach in a protected vehicle with a barricade phone. Toss it in and start negotiations. We'll need the building plans."

"Sounds good," Emily yelled over the reverberating rotor wash of the helicopter. "Except Mooney's been flawlessly cold-blooded up to this point. I can't believe for a second he wants to negotiate a damn thing."

A female cop came over with an ashen-faced woman in her seventies.

"Cap," the officer said. "This is the school secretary. She saw the guy who's holding the kids."

"He killed Coach Webb," she blurted between hysterical sobs. "He shot Coach Webb in the face."

That was it. That sealed it. He'd already started shooting. All-too-familiar gory school-shooting news footage flashed through my mind. No way. No goddamn way.

Without further deliberation, I decided on a course of action.

I started sprinting for the arched entrance of St. Edward's.

Chapter 83

"MIKE! WAIT! WHAT the hell are you doing?" Emily called behind me.

"I'm going to end this," I yelled over my shoulder as I cleared my gun. "One way or another. Right now."

Glock firmly in hand, I burst through the school's front door in a combat crouch. My overtaxed heart felt like it was about to burst as well when the door rattled shut behind me.

In the glass trophy case beside me were spooky sepia photographs of smiling St. Edward's students from the turn of the century. I took a deep breath and bit my lip as I peered down the long, even spookier empty corridor in front of me.

"Not so fast, Bennett," Emily whispered, coming in behind me.

Even better, the eight members of the Hostage Rescue Team were right behind her.

"Stay stacked and watch those corners," Chow whispered into his tactical mic as they cut ahead. "Off the wall, Jennings bullets tend to ricochet, remember? Guns and eyeballs, people. Make me look bad, and I'll kick your tail."

The obsessively trained commandos began making sure the classrooms were empty. Fast crossing thresholds, they kept low so as not to silhouette themselves from inside.

We found the body of Coach Webb in the Admissions office three minutes later. He'd been shot once in the head. A mix of fury and sadness sizzled through me as I stared down at the cross-shaped wound in his skull. Almost like ashes, I thought.

I was looking at Mooney's twisted version of Ash Wednesday.

We were coming back out into the hall when a loud thundering sound started. The door at the other end of the corridor flew open wide. I swallowed and sucked breath at the same time.

"Hold your fire!" I yelled.

It was the kids. Students in navy blazers, hundreds

of them, were running toward us out of the gym, obviously in a panic. Many of them were crying as they rushed down the hall at full speed.

I scanned the crowd for Mooney, for explosives or a gun. He wasn't there. What now? And what the hell? He was letting them go?

We directed the kids toward the front entrance and radioed outside that they were coming out. When the last one made it to the front foyer, we continued down the hallway, running now for the gym.

"Freeze!" Chow yelled to a shocked-looking man coming around the stands.

"Please! I'm the headmaster. Henry Joyce," the distraught bald man said. "He's taken two of the students. Jeremy Mason and Aidan Parrish. He called them out and handcuffed them together before telling everyone to run. There was nothing I could do.... Oh, God!"

He pointed to a door at the opposite side of the basketball court.

"I think he took them into the basement."

Chapter 84

ON THE OTHER side of the gym's parquet, I hit the basement door at a full-court sprint. I was only half a step ahead of Emily. The HRT guys were at our backs as we went down the cement stairs two by two.

The basement was dark and stifling and smelled like chlorine. Would he try to kill the two boys down here before we got to him? Had he already? A boiler roared as we passed some industrial equipment for the school's pool.

I saw a slanting ray of daylight as we turned a corner. It was coming down from an open cellar grate in the ceiling. I jumped up a short steel ladder that headed up the hatch and poked my Glock out. When I didn't get shot, I stuck my head out.

Goddammit! There was a short Dumpster-filled alley to my right. The alley had a steel gate at its end. An *open* steel gate, which led out onto 80th Street at the back end of the blockwide school campus.

From around the corner came a yell and a squeal of tires.

"Shit! C'mon!" I yelled to Emily as I climbed out onto the cracked cement.

A shocked-looking Filipino taxi driver wearing a white Kangol hat was standing in the street with a cell phone to his ear. A group of construction workers behind him were pointing east toward Lexington Avenue.

"He just turned right onto Lex," the cabbie said as he saw the badge around my neck. "Some crazy son of a bitch just jacked my taxi."

"Were there kids with him?" I yelled as I ran past.

"Two of them," the Filipino said. "They were handcuffed together. What the hell just happened?"

I wish I knew, I thought as I booked down the middle of the street.

I turned the corner and stood for a moment, dazed and staring. Lexington Avenue was filled with trucks, buses, cars, and taxis.

Dozens and dozens of taxis were flowing south into

the distance by the second. None of them seemed to be speeding or acting erratically. There was no way to tell which one was Mooney's!

I was pulling out my cell to call for a roadblock, when it rang in my hand.

"Mike? It's me," a calm, educated voice said.

Mooney! I couldn't speak. Sweat poured off me while I fought to catch my breath. Horns honked at me as I waded out even farther into traffic, craning my neck down the block to see if he would reveal where he was. Was he going to taunt me now? Rub it in that he got away? I'd even take a shot from him at this point just to get an inkling of where he was.

Emily arrived at the corner with a where-the-hell-is-he expression on her face.

"Francis?" I said, pointing at my phone.

"If anyone tries to stop me, the two boys will die."

"Nobody wants that to happen," I said. "Listen, Francis. We know about the Ash Wednesday bombing where your friends died. That wasn't your fault, man. Don't blame yourself for that. You did the right thing. I heard about your cancer, too. That sucks.

"We also know about the charity work and pro bono stuff. You're a good guy. Why do you want this to be your legacy? These are defenseless kids. How does this make sense?"

"Who says that the world has to make sense, Mike? Besides, my legacy doesn't matter," he said after a pause. "Only one thing matters."

I felt like bashing the phone off my skull. What was it with this guy? He sounded messianic, as if he thought he was on a mission from God.

"Why?" I yelled. "Why the hell are you doing this?"

"You're Catholic, right, Mike? Of course you are. What New York Irish cop isn't? Did you hear the Gospel today? Did you *listen* to the Gospel? If you had, you wouldn't be asking me that question."

The Gospel?!

"Take me, then, Francis. Take me in place of the kids. Whatever you need to do, you can use me instead."

"That wouldn't work, Mike. You'll see. It will all be revealed to you. To everyone. It's not long now. I'm almost at my final destination. *Our* final destination. This is almost over. Relieved? I am."

He sobbed then. Funny, but I didn't feel sorry for him at all, despite his obviously fragile emotional state.

"This is the worst thing anyone has ever done. But that's okay. I'm probably the only one strong enough to do it."

Chapter 85

MOONEY ZIPPED THROUGH the Lexington Avenue traffic quickly, but not too quickly. Cutting off a FedEx truck, he skillfully made a hairpin right onto 57th Street.

He hadn't planned to carjack the taxi. He actually had a rental car parked in an underground lot behind St. Edward's. But when he saw the taxi just sitting there in traffic, as if waiting for him, he seized the opportunity.

He now had the two students gagged and double-cuffed down on the floor. Mason was blond, and Parrish had reddish-brown hair, but the two seniors could have been brothers. Handsome, athletic-looking, and oh-so-elite in their Burberry shirts and Polo ties.

The question wasn't where they'd be going to college, Mooney knew. The question was, which Ivy League school? An eye-popping twenty-five percent of the students at St. Edward's went on to Ivy League schools. In some city public schools, fewer than twenty-five percent even graduated.

The inequality didn't end there, of course. Parrish's father was CEO of Mellon Zaxo, the household-product giant. He'd been the third-highest-compensated executive in the United States the year before, with over one hundred and thirteen million dollars in salary and stock bonuses. Mason's dad was the North American chief of Takia, the monolithic Russian natural gas corporation. He'd just squeaked into the top ten by raking in a paltry sixty-one million.

This, while the average American household income topped off at fifty-three thousand. While regular people went without health insurance and lost their houses in banking subprime swindles.

A groan came from the backseat.

"One more stop, now, fellas," Mooney called to them.

A short stop, he thought, but vitally important.

He slowed as he arrived at the Four Seasons Hotel on the corner of 57th and Park Avenue. The opulent fifty-two-story I. M. Pei–designed midtown landmark was a favorite with movie stars and billionaires.

A handsome college-age doorman in a nineteenth-century-inspired uniform and a top hat raced out through the brass revolving door.

Popping open the taxi's rear door, the hotel worker stood there in his ridiculous footman's uniform, staring stupefied at the two students handcuffed on the floor of the backseat.

Mooney leaned through the divider and pressed the Beretta to the doorman's square jaw.

The male-model look-alike took a wad of ones from his pocket.

"Take it, bro. All yours," he said.

Mooney pistol-whipped the bills out of the young man's white-gloved hands.

"Get in now," he said.

"What?" the doorman said. "Get in? Me?"

"Yes, get in the front seat or I'll put a bullet in your chest. How's that for a tip? I won't tell you twice," Mooney said as he unlocked the front door.

Chapter 86

TWENTY MINUTES LATER, Mooney let out a sigh of relief as he reached Canal Street. He made a left and then a quick right two blocks east onto Mott. He stomped down on the accelerator, barreling the Chevy taxicab down the narrow, winding Chinatown street.

He'd made it. He was in the maze of downtown now. This was going to happen. Absolutely nothing could stop him now.

Mooney found the Bowery and took it to St. James Place and farther south onto Pearl. He thought he would feel nervous as he neared his final destination, but it was the exact opposite. He'd never felt so elated, so clean. He was coming into contact with the sublime now.

Stopping the stolen taxi on Pearl half a block north of Beaver, Mooney looked out on the compact downtown skyline. Austere modern glass cliff faces squeezed between soaring Beaux Arts granite facades. An entire vista built by greed, he thought. By evil and slavery and war.

Was it any wonder that, even before the two attacks on the World Trade Center, the area had retained such a violent, bloody history? The 1970 Hard Hat Riot, where hundreds of thug blue-collar workers severely beat the members of an antiwar demonstration. The 1975 Fraunces Tavern bombing by the Puerto Rican separatist group FALN, which had killed four people. As far back as 1920, a wagon loaded with iron slugs and a hundred pounds of dynamite had been set off by anarchists in front of the New York Stock Exchange, killing thirty-three people.

History really does repeat itself, Francis thought as he opened his bag.

He began to methodically prepare the boys and doorman and himself. Wordlessly, he stepped out with them onto the sidewalk. A pudgy Asian businesswoman coming out of an Au Bon Pain in front of them screamed before throwing herself back inside.

Francis gazed at the monstrous American flag draped down the massive Corinthian columns of the Stock Exchange's famous Neoclassical facade. He looked at the maze of steel barricades and concrete car stops that provided blast cushion, to use the parlance of counterterror circles. There was about a regiment of heavily armed law enforcement on the sidewalk. They stood beside Emergency Service panel trucks, holding rifles and black telescope-like Geiger counters. He was supposed to get by them?

A snatch of Nietzsche came to him, comforted him.

He who has a why to live can bear almost any how.

Mooney and the three young men were turning the corner of Exchange Place and Broad when the bomb dogs started up. He was linked to the men with strand upon strand of the det cord and strips of plastic explosive. Tangled together in the thick clothesline-like explosive, they looked strange and terrifying, a cross between performance artists and victims of a construction accident.

The cocking of automatic rifles from the SWAT cops behind the steel barricades rang down the narrow trench of the street as Francis shuffled toward them, connected to the two boys and the doorman. The police were converging on him as he made it to the barricade closest to the Exchange's corner employee entrance.

An older, pugnacious-looking buzz-cut cop in a suit and trench coat was the first to reach them. His name was Dennis Quinn, and he was the Stock Exchange's security chief for the day shift. Francis knew all about him, had done hours of extensive research on the man, in fact.

Quinn had served ten years in the Marine Corps and another twenty in the FBI before landing the well-paying Exchange security job. The middle-aged man yelled into a collar mic as he drew a Ruger .40 caliber and pointed it at Mooney's head.

"I'd watch where I pointed that thing, if I were you," Francis said with a smile. "I wouldn't want you to hurt anyone." He indicated the doorman tangled beside him to the right.

"Most especially your son here, Dennis."

The gun in Quinn's hand trembled as he looked at the doorman for the first time.

"Oh, my God! Kevin?" Quinn said.

Francis raised his hands with the electronic detonator controller taped between them. He showed Quinn where his thumb was taped down to the detonator's charge button.

"See the indicator light? The det cord? The plastic?

We're charged and ready to go, Dennis. All I have to do is pull the trigger."

Dennis Quinn's Adam's apple did a hard bob as he thought about that.

Francis stared dead into the man's eyes.

"It's simple. I die, we all die. You, me, these two young men here. Oh, and your only son. I know you're a patriot, Dennis. Rah-rah, nine/eleven, never forget, and all that. But are you actually willing to kill your only son? Are you that crazy? Because that's exactly what's going to happen if you don't move the barricades to the side and let me through that door.

"This is a test, Dennis. You can protect either A, those heartless, money-worshipping savages inside that building behind you, or B, your son. One or the other. Not both. What is it going to be?"

Chapter 87

AFTER MOONEY HUNG up on me, I ran as fast as I could back to the main entrance at St. Edward's. On the way, I called for a roadblock on Lexington and for Aviation to keep an eye south on Lex for erratically driving taxis. That was pretty much asking for them to keep an eye out for water in the ocean, so I wasn't too hopeful. In fact, after the most recent events and Mooney's messianic nutball monologue, I was deep in full-despair territory.

A lot of blond, ladies-who-lunch, Upper East Side moms were now embracing their kids by the Park Avenue median. Other worried-looking parents were breathlessly waiting by the police sawhorses, yelling and gazing into the crowd of released schoolkids.

Were Mason's and Parrish's mothers waiting there? I wondered.

"Bomb Squad and the Hostage Rescue guys are still inside, securing the building," Emily told me as she cupped her cell. "They're searching for booby traps, making sure Mooney hasn't left any of the explosive behind."

"I'm more afraid that he hasn't," I said, dialing my boss. "In fact, I'm much more afraid that he's taken every ounce of it with him and those two poor kids."

EMTs were bringing out the body of Coach Webb as my phone rang. No one else had been hurt, thank God.

At least not yet.

The young black Nineteenth Precinct captain rushed over to me, holding his cell phone toward me.

"Detective, it's Commissioner Daly."

"Bennett," I said into it.

"Mike, it's John Daly. Listen, bad news. Mooney just arrived out in front of the Stock Exchange. He's wired himself to three people with the plastic explosive and is insisting on going inside."

I closed my eyes, resisting the urge to start screaming. The New York Stock Exchange? And what did he just say?

"Three people?!" I said. "He only abducted two St. Edward's kids as far as we can tell."

"I heard it was three, Mike. Just get down there with Agent Parker and the Hostage Rescue Team ASAP and see what you can do. You guys know him best."

Yeah, I thought, handing the captain back his phone. That was the problem. I knew all too well what Mooney was all about.

I frantically waved over the Hostage Rescue and Bomb Squad guys.

"Where to now?" Emily said with a pained look on her face as we hopped back into her car. "I'm running out of gas."

"Financial district. Where else?" I said. "Mooney just showed up at the Stock Exchange."

Chapter 88

SHACKLED TO THE three young men with high explosives, Francis X. Mooney stutter-stepped through the grand lobby of 11 Wall Street. Though the dozen NYPD and private Stock Exchange officers stationed there had guns trained at his head, they parted before him as he led his captives toward the metal detectors.

The officers kept pace half a step behind them like paparazzi with guns instead of cameras.

Francis's heart beat in a way he'd never experienced before, like a bass drum at the end of a German opera. Fear and ecstasy commingled in his blood into something terrible and wonderful, something entirely new. He knew Quinn's kid had been the deciding factor.

He'd done the impossible. *He was actually inside the New York Stock Exchange!*

The Parrish boy tripped on some of the det cord and fell. Francis turned with a smile and gently helped him up off the polished stone.

"It's not much further now, son. I promise," he said.

Around the corner in the middle of the right-hand wall, he halted by the door he wanted. It led up some stairs to a door to the balcony above the trading floor where they rang the opening bell.

He'd been here once before. A client of his was going public with his biotech company, and Mooney had been invited to attend the ceremony. He'd stood behind the executive, smiling and clapping obediently, as the old-fashioned plate bell clanged the new trading day.

How many men had he helped to amass staggering amounts of unfair wealth? he thought. Too many to count. That's why he was here. He was making up for that. For all of it.

He turned and faced the officers at his heels.

"We're going through that door now. Alone. After I'm inside, I'm going to seal it with explosives. Follow and everyone dies. Thank you."

Mooney opened the door, pulled the three young men through, then sealed it with PE-4. The explosive was pretty much useless because it wasn't attached to a detonator, but how would they know that? It would deter them enough.

The yelling from the cavernous trading floor was palpable as they opened the door at the top of the stairs. He led the boys out onto the end of the balcony.

On the pompous granite walls hung huge American flags and neon blue NYSE banners. Every three feet, it seemed, was some kind of computer screen. On them scrolled the relentless march of numbers showing the ever-changing stock bids.

Below was pandemonium, a confusing mosh pit of men and women in business suits and colored smocks. They were yelling and typing into small computers hanging around their necks as they crowded by the carousel-like stock-trading desks. He stared down at the pathetic scurrying, the little ants scrambling for their crumbs. They'd thank him for this.

Mooney stepped up on the podium that stood by the balcony's railing for the celebrities who rang the opening bell. He flicked the microphone on and thumped it with his taped-up hands.

"Stop!" Mooney yelled out over the trading floor.

A scary hush went through the chamber as traders and brokers stopped what they were doing and craned upward.

Mooney was weeping again. He was surprised to see that some of the traders on the floor had ashes on their foreheads. Were they really ready to share in the world's suffering? To sacrifice themselves?

He took a deep breath.

Time to find out, he thought.

Chapter 89

THE MIDTOWN TRAFFIC had never seemed more impassable while Emily and I tried to carve a path downtown. Minute after precious minute slipped away as we screeched and slanted our way down Lexington through Turtle Bay and Murray Hill, the Flat Iron district, Gramercy Park, Union Square.

"So many neighborhoods, so little damn time," I yelled with my ear cocked to the radio for the worst.

We were coming into SoHo when my phone rang. Was it over?

"Mooney just forced his way inside the Stock Exchange," Chief Fleming told me.

"Wh—, wh—, what?" I screamed. "How the hell did he manage that!"

I couldn't believe it. The security around the Stock Exchange had to be the highest in the city, maybe in the world. It seemed like all of southern Manhattan was one huge blockade after 9/11.

"Right after he snatched the St. Edward's kids, the son of a bitch took the Exchange's security chief's kid from his doorman job at gunpoint. Then Mooney tangled himself, the students, and the doorman all together with the missing det cord and explosives. Dennis Quinn, the security chief, was manning the employee entrance when Mooney showed up, threatening to blow up his kid right on the street if Quinn didn't let him inside. Quinn let him in. What the hell else was he supposed to do? It doesn't matter now, does it?"

It sounded like Emily removed the muffler when she scraped the Crown Vic up onto the curb in front of Trinity Church six minutes later. Hopping out, I almost knocked down Chief Fleming, who was standing next to the NYPD Critical Incident bus, parked across the length of Broadway.

"Mooney's blocked himself off in the balcony above the trading floor where they ring the opening bell," my boss said over the wail of sirens that seemed to be coming from every direction. "He also just called nine-one-one. He's made an offer. He says he'll exchange the St. Edward's students for their fathers. We have thirty minutes to get them here. We're contacting them now."

My head spun. Mooney was willing to exchange the kids for their fathers but not for me? Emily and I scrambled to put it together.

"You kidnap two rich kids, bring them down here, and now you want their fathers?" Emily said. "Why not just grab them? Mooney's a proven freaking mastermind at snatching people."

How did any of it make sense? And what the hell did the son of a bitch really want?

"What about the people on the trading floor?" I said.

"A lot of them got out. But there's still maybe three hundred financial workers holed up behind the trading desks. Except for the stairwell to the balcony, he hasn't sealed any doors, thank God."

Chief Fleming led us down the block toward the employee entrance at the corner of Broad and Wall. Task force uniforms and tactical cops had taken up positions on both sides of the street. Beneath the giant American flag on the face of the landmark building, scared-shitless-looking brokers and traders in colored smocks and ID necklaces were being evacuated north up Broad Street.

"Snipers?" Emily said.

"That's the rub," my boss said. "He's got the detonator taped to his hands. Even with a head shot, Mooney could still manage to pull the trigger."

We hurried back up to Broadway once the FBI's Hostage Rescue Team truck arrived. Even superstoic Chow seemed subdued as he stared down the world-famous narrow trench of Wall Street.

He pointed to an overhead satellite map of the Financial district he already had up on the Power-Point screen.

"All right. First thing we need to do is get that giant flag down off the front of the building. My sniper observers are heading into this office building across Broad Street here. These long windows between the columns on the edifice of the Exchange look onto the trading floor. I place the balcony where Mooney is holed up about fifteen feet to the right of this central window. If we can get him to move maybe even ten feet back, we can blow out the window and angle a shot at him."

"What about the fact that the detonator is taped to his hands?" Fleming said.

"We're going to use an extremely high-velocity Barrett M107 fifty-caliber sniper rifle. Coupled with a nonincendiary sabot round, we should be able to minimize collateral damage. We'll go for the detonator itself before he gets a chance to set it off."

Emily and I stared at each other, shaking our heads in dismay. What were the odds of coming away from this thing without more loss of life?

"I know," Chow said. "It's not pretty by any stretch, but it's the only tactical play we have."

Chapter 90

THAT DISMAL NEWS was still ringing loudly in our ears as the St. Edward's students' fathers showed up in a squad car.

Tall and fair with graying executive hair, Howard Parrish looked like a CEO out of central casting. I recognized his face from the tabloids due to a very messy divorce he'd gone through the year before. Edwin Mason, short, dark, and wearing glasses, had more of a professorial air in his jeans and sports coat.

"What the hell is this about, my boy? Tell me this instant!" Parrish said by way of greeting as he stepped onto the NYPD's Critical Incident bus.

"Howard's right. Could someone please give us

the straight story?" Edwin Mason said with a pleading calm.

"Your boys are being held hostage in the Stock Exchange by a man named Francis Mooney," I said bluntly. "He's the man who's responsible for abducting and killing several wealthy young adults in the past four days."

Parrish's face went hypertension-tomato-red.

"That damned school sent home a bulletin just yesterday about beefed-up security. How could this be allowed to happen? And why my boy? There's hundreds of kids at that school. Why mine?"

"There's more to it than that, isn't there?" Mason said, looking steadily into my eyes. "You're leaving something out."

"There is more to it," I said. "Mooney contacted us a few minutes ago. He said he's willing to do an exchange. Your boys for you."

"For us?" Parrish said, bamboozled. "You mean he wants to hold us hostage instead? Why?"

"In addition to being obviously unstable, Mooney has a radical-left history that goes back to the sixties," Emily said. "Bottom line, he's extremely dissatisfied with wealthy people. There's a whole quasi-political motive wrapped up in his actions. At least, that's what he seems to believe."

"Goddamn liberals!" Parrish said, his voice cracking. "The goddamn liberals are actually going to kill my son!"

Mason took off his glasses and put them back on again.

"Does why really matter, Howard?" he said wearily. "Our boys are in real trouble."

"We're doing all we can to resolve this," I cut in. "It's entirely up to you how you want to play things. We can't force you to exchange yourselves. We can't even advise it. There's no way to guarantee your safety. But if you volunteer, we won't get in your way. In fact, during the exchange, we might be able to create an opportunity to resolve things."

"Volunteering isn't a choice," Mason said after a second. "My wife died six years ago. My son is the only thing I treasure in this world. Send me in."

Chewing on a pinkie nail, Parrish stared at the bus floor between his wingtips, deliberating for a few moments.

"Yes, okay," he finally said. "Me, too. Send me in, too, of course."

Chapter 91

MY HEART WENT out to the two CEOs as we exchanged their coats for bulletproof vests. Many parents believe that they would gladly give up their lives for their children's, but these men were actually being given the choice. The simple, staggering courage they were showing blew me and every other cop in the room away.

"I don't want to die, Edwin," Parrish said as his eyes welled with tears. He seemed to be speaking more to himself than to anyone there. "But hey, I've led a good life. Been really, really fortunate. I always tried to do my best. And if I do go, at least my money will go to my boy and a good cause: the AIDS Research Alliance."

"Well said, Howard," Edwin Mason agreed, squeezing Parrish's shoulder. "That's the right way to look at things. My dough is destined for Amfar. Millions of people will benefit from what we achieved."

Wait a second, I thought. Charities again? Something suddenly occurred to me.

"Who does your legal work, Mr. Mason? Who did your will?" I said.

"Ericsson, Weymouth and Roth," Mason said.

I don't know whose eyes went wider at the mention of Mooney's firm, Emily's or mine.

"That's funny. Small world. Mine, too," said Parrish.

Emily and I faded into the corner of the bus.

"Charities? Wills?" she said. "This is definitely connected. Mooney was the head of Trusts and Estates, wasn't he?"

"Wait a second. Damn it!" I said. "There was something Mooney said in our last conversation. Something about the Ash Wednesday Gospel."

I whipped out my cell and speed-dialed Seamus. Sometimes having a priest in the family came in handy.

"Listen up. I need your help here, Seamus," I said. "No monkeying around. Today's Gospel. Read me today's Gospel."

"Don't tell me you weren't listening? Remind me to box your ears next time we meet, ye heathen. Okay, I have it right here. Let's see. Matthew six, one to four: 'Beware of your practicing your piety before men in order to be seen by them. For then you will have no reward from your Father who is in heaven. Thus, when you give alms, do not sound the trumpet before you, as the hypocrites do in the synagogues and the streets that they may be praised by men. Truly, I say unto you, they have received their reward. But when you give alms, do not let your left hand know what your right hand is doing, so that your alms may be in secret, and your Father who sees what is in secret will reward you.' "

"Wait a second. Read that back about the alms."

" 'That your alms may be in secret,' " Seamus said.

That was it!

I grabbed Emily as I slapped the phone closed.

"I got it! Mooney's giving alms in secret!"

"Giving what?" Emily said, confused.

"Alms. Charity. Don't you see? In every case, the family had a philanthropic bent. And in every case, the child was the sole beneficiary of mega wealth. When Mooney learned he was going to die, he concocted this whole thing as a way to cut out the child and donate as much money as he could directly to charity!"

Emily stood there with her mouth open.

"That clever little weasel. That explains the deal with the tests he gave the kids. He was trying to see if they were socially conscious enough to be allowed to inherit their parents' wealth. That explains why he let the Haas girl live. But how does that help us now?"

"I'll tell you how," I said. "Mooney doesn't want to exchange the fathers for the kids. He's not going to exchange anything. Mason and Parrish are both single. Once Mooney sees the fathers, he's going to kill all of them. The fathers, the sons, and himself. The money won't even have to wait for the fathers' natural lifetimes to expire in order for it to go to charity. It'll happen right now."

Carol Fleming came over.

"What's the story, guys? Are we sending the fathers in or not?"

"No way, boss," I said. "But I think I have a plan."

Chapter 92

"LET'S TALK ABOUT the horrors of the modern world that the greed in this room has helped to create," Mooney said into the balcony microphone.

"Let's go over the crimes that all of you here have helped to perpetrate. The environmental travesties, the worker exploitation and deaths, the public corruption and tax evasion. Do you care about the black lung and asbestosis that your corporate masters inflict on their workers? The pollution that your holy shareholders and investors condone?"

Mooney looked down at their blank faces.

"I was like you. I slaved for the corporate machine, protecting it from the law in ways regular people will never be privy to. Protected illegal price fixes and unethical policies against millions of regular working-class people. I saw crimes of unthinkable magnitude. I saw pristine waterways irrevocably befouled with pollution. No one was held responsible. No one went to jail. Why is that? Can anyone tell me?

"By the way, I can see that many of you here are grossly overweight. But what percentage of the world's population is starving as we have our little talk here? Anyone have the answer? Don't be shy."

Chapter 93

IT TOOK US five minutes to confer with my boss and the Hostage Rescue Team chief Tom Chow. Chow made the final arrangements over his tactical mic as Emily and I pulled on ceramic bomb vests.

"What's the story now, Detective?" Howard Parrish said as we emerged from the bus. "We're not going in now? What about my boy?"

"Something new has come to light. It's our best chance to resolve this thing without any more innocent people getting hurt. We're going to do the best we can, sir," Emily said.

"That's not good enough. Fuck that! I want my son alive. If you can't guarantee that, then I want to go instead of him. I demand to!"

I stopped and held the executive by his elbow.

"Listen to me, Mr. Parrish," I said. "I guarantee you that I will bring your son back to you alive."

We walked away.

"What the hell are you doing, Mike? How can you make a promise like that?" Emily said under her breath as we headed down Wall Street toward the Stock Exchange entrance.

"Easy," I said, shrugging my shoulders. "If things go south, I won't be around for him to yell at me."

Chow met us at the security barricades and briefed us a final time while we walked through the maze of steel.

"Everything is in place," he finally said, stopping by the Exchange's door. "The rest is up to you two."

Emily and I passed the metal detectors in the huge empty lobby. We walked silently, thinking our own thoughts as we stepped down the hall.

"Good luck, Detective Bennett. This works, I'll buy you dinner," Emily said as I stopped by the door that led to the balcony stairwell.

"Hope you brought your American Express card, Agent Parker," I said as she continued on, heading for the trading floor. "Because if this works, I'm planning on about fifteen before-dinner drinks."

Chapter 94

COMING DOWN THE hall, Parker was grateful for the speed with which all this was happening. There was no time to think. Which was good. If she'd had to think about things, she knew she'd be walking in the opposite direction.

A couple of Stock Exchange cops were crouched by the last security station, staring through the window of the entrance to the trading floor. Parker badged them.

"Where is he?"

A couple of brokers cringing behind the trading desks whispered loudly.

"Watch it, lady. That guy's nuts."

"He's got a gun," a pudgy white guy with thinning black hair told her.

She stepped out into the space.

"You actually thought you'd get away with it, didn't you, shit for brains! Yes, I'm talking to you, scumbag!"

"Who are you?" Mooney called over the microphone.

"Me? I'm a moral person who went to work today," Emily screamed. "You, on the other hand, are a common murderer, a killer of children, a serial killer, and probably a pervert."

"Hey, lady!" one of the brokers said. "Shut up! You're going to get us all killed!"

"I am not!" Mooney yelled.

"I am not!" Emily said, mimicking him. "Who are you kidding? You got off on killing every one of those kids."

"Those *kids,* as you call them, were worthless, useless. They deserved to die!" Mooney screamed. "Their parents should have educated them better. Should have taught them the importance of being human."

"Oh, you're teaching all of us humanity?" Emily screamed. "My mistake. I thought you were just *killing children!*"

Chapter 95

CHECKING MY WATCH, I knelt down next to the tactical "mouse hole" the HRT guys had already made into the hallway wall to avoid the explosives. At the top of the narrow stairs, I unscrewed the fluorescent light and laid it down carefully on the dusty, worn marble tiles and slowly opened the door.

About twenty feet away with his back to me, Mooney stood at the front railing of the balcony with his captives, yelling down at Emily. Between us, dividing the balcony in half at an angle, was a five-foot-wide stripe of bright sunlight that fell from the Stock Exchange's front window. I stared at the light intently for a moment before I opened my mouth.

"Francis! Over here! Hey, don't listen to her!" I called to him.

Mooney swung around toward me, angry and confused. He shook the detonator at me.

"You're sneaking up on me? Try something, and I'll do it!" he screamed. "Right now. I'll do everyone! Where are the fathers? Why is no one listening to me?"

I stared fearfully at the two high school kids and the security chief's son, all of whom Mooney had bound himself to. They were pale, listless, sweating, eyes glazed with stress and shock. I thought of my oldest boy, Brian, only a few years younger. I wanted them to live. I wanted us all to live. I had to make this happen. Somehow.

"Francis! Calm down, man! It's me, Mike Bennett," I said, raising my hands slowly above my head. "I'm not sneaking up on you. I have the fathers in the hall here behind me, like you said. I'll let them in. You let the boys go. Will you work with me?"

Mooney took a step toward me. His eyes behind his glasses were gleaming now, filled with an unsettling intensity. His taped-together hands holding the detonator were shaking now. I watched his right-hand index finger twitch as it hovered over its trigger.

I struggled to come up with something to calm

him down. Emily's tirade was supposed to be just a distraction, but it had gotten him so riled up, he might set the plastic off by accident.

"Where are they?" Mooney demanded, peering into the darkened doorway at my back.

"At the bottom of the stairwell, Francis. They're waiting to come up," I said.

"You're lying," Mooney said.

"No," I said, making eye contact with him as I shook my head. "No more lies, Francis. We just want what's best for everybody. For you. For those kids. The fathers really want to take their sons' places. They appreciate that you've given them the option, in fact."

"Yeah, like I believe that," Mooney said. He took another step closer, his eyes squinting as he tried to peer deeper into the dim stairwell.

"I won't let anyone go until the fathers come up those stairs and stand in front of me. That's the deal, Mike. No negotiating. Bring them up here right now."

I turned around as if I heard something behind me.

"Okay, Francis," I said. "They're on the stairs right behind me now. Why don't we do this? Why don't you come forward a little and look in the doorway first. You can verify that it's them. Then you can untangle one of the kids. I don't want you to think it's a trick."

Mooney stood there, thinking about it.

"Okay," he said, taking another step.

As he came forward, I watched the sunlight from the window glance off his shoe. The light came up his leg, his torso, his two hands grasping the detonator as if in prayer.

"Got him," the FBI sniper across the street said into the radio in my ear.

I dove to the floor.

Chapter 96

STANDING IN THE dusty light, Mooney looked at me in confusion as I hit the deck. Then he turned toward the window I'd lured him in front of.

The shattering of the long front window of the Exchange seemed to happen after Mooney was hit. One second, he was standing there, and the next, the window shattered spectacularly, and he was down, sitting on the floor.

The blood pumping from Mooney's wrists looked black on the bright faded marble. I scrambled up as Mooney fruitlessly tried to squeeze the detonator trigger. He was having trouble because his blown-apart hands and wrists were now only barely attached to his arms.

The .50 caliber sniper bullets had missed the detonator but hit him through both wrists, completely severing the nerves in both hands.

I felt sorry for Mooney as he wriggled on the floor, moaning and pumping blood.

But that was before he whispered, "Amen," and lurched up and forward, going for the trigger with his chin.

The third shot came before I'd closed half the distance. The final bullet caught Mooney on his temple. Instead of falling forward, he fell over safely to the side.

"Cease fire!" I yelled into my radio as a thunder of steps came up the balcony stairs.

"No!" I screamed at Jeremy Mason, who'd turned to look at what was left of Francis X. Mooney.

I knelt down in front of the young man tangled in the strings of explosives, shielding him from the sight of Mooney's body. He'd been through enough. We all had.

"Don't move, son. It's going to be okay now," I said, wiping at the madman's blood freckled across the boy's face.

Chapter 97

I WAS TRYING to extricate the boys when one of the bomb techs tackled me from behind and shoved me back toward the stairs.

The St. Edward's students came down less than five minutes later. Both of the dads were crying openly as they met them in the building's foyer. Even the burly security chief, Quinn, sobbed as he wrapped his arms around his doorman son, who appeared a few minutes later.

The cops and brokers crowded outside on Broad Street broke into a cheer as the fathers and sons came out. Someone started up a chant of *U-S-A* for some reason. Relieved that we were both still alive, Emily and I hugged before heartily joining in.

It took the bomb techs half an hour to secure and remove the explosives. After they left, I went back up to the balcony with Emily and the Crime Scene guys. Head shots are horrible, and this one was no exception. Mooney had actually been shot out of his shoes. I stared at the bloody gouges the .50 caliber rounds had also taken out of the old building's stone walls. Mooney had made an impact, all right.

I stood there silently with Emily as the medical examiner zippered the body bag closed.

"Check this out," one of the CSU guys said, coming up to me with a sheet of paper in a plastic evidence bag. "It was stuffed into the pocket of Mooney's jacket."

WARNING TO A WORLD ON THE EVE OF DESTRUCTION was its title. It was a litany of what was wrong with the world. Facts about poverty and famine and disease. Across the bottom, Mooney had scribbled NO ONE IS LISTENING! in red pen.

Emily lifted an eyebrow at me as I removed the sheet from the plastic. I tore it in half. Then in half again.

"That bastard invalidated everything he had to say the second he started hurting innocent people," I said, ripping it a third time. "Screw his message, whether it's true or false. I'll take C, none of the above."

I felt Parker's hand on the back of my neck as I tossed the ripped paper off the balcony.

"Amen, Mike," she said as the torn pieces disappeared among the stock tickets that littered the floor.

Chapter 98

EMILY GOT OFF easy. She didn't have to buy dinner that night after all. Parrish and Mason got together and insisted on throwing a dinner for the entire task force at none other than the famous Tavern on the Green on Central Park West.

They rented out one of the small dining rooms for the nearly one hundred cops who showed up. Schultz and Ramirez, who'd arrived early to the open bar, looked like they were into double-digit Bellinis. Most likely looking at a pay-grade increase, they wrapped their arms around each other when the hired ten-piece swing band started playing "New York, New York."

"*I want to wake up in a city that doesn't sleep,*" they sang, Rockette-kicking in front of the laughing tuxedoed musicians. *"To find I'm A number one, top of the list, king of the hill."*

"See, I keep telling you this department is one class act," I said, taking Emily by the hand. I danced her around the room with its crystal chandeliers and hand-carved mirrors. When we weren't dancing, we drank. Champagne, of course. By the time we sat down to dinner, we were laughing deliriously, too loudly probably, and not caring in the slightest.

The waiters were all over us in a way I'd never experienced before. French champagne glass after French champagne glass. Out of curiosity, I peeked at the menu and noticed that they were three- and four hundred dollars a bottle.

"What you did at the Exchange took guts, Emily," I said, tossing back another thirty-dollar glass. "You really looked good in there."

Veuve Clicquot suddenly sprayed from my nose as Parker found my thigh under the table.

"Isn't that a coincidence?" she said, staring into my eyes as she knocked back her own glass. "You look good in here, Detective."

Emily and I both sprinted through the dinner for some reason. Our spoons clacked on the tiramisu plates before most of the cops at our table had even started.

"Where are you guys going?" my boss asked as we said our quick good-byes. "You're the stars of the party. Parrish and Mason haven't even gotten here yet."

"Uh," I said, "Emily has to, uh..."

"Catch a flight," she finished for me. "Got to get home tonight. Back down to DC. Boy, I can't miss that plane."

The taxi ride back to Emily's hotel was hot and heavy and way too short. It consisted of what every perfect New York City evening is made—the swirling Times Square lights, silk, nylon, sharp red nails, a grinning, envious cabbie.

We almost knocked down a high school senior class from Missouri as we speed-walked to the hotel's elevator. The elevator door was closing when I stuck out my arm at the last second. The door rolled back open.

"What the hell are you doing?" Emily said.

"I just remembered something," I said tentatively.

"It's the nanny, isn't it?"

I didn't say anything.

"It is, Mike. It's definitely the nanny, whether you realize it or not. Oh, well."

She kissed me for the last time then. She grabbed my lapel and slammed her lips into mine viciously.

She seemed so warm this close. I wanted to get closer. I don't think I can properly express how much I wanted to ride that elevator up.

Then Emily even more viciously shoved me away from her. She actually kicked me in the knee with a high heel to get me moving out of the elevator car.

"Your loss, cop," she spat, extremely pissed and extremely hot with her blouse tails out, her flushed cheeks, and red hair mussed. "Your fucking loss, Bennett, you goddamn asshole."

My breath went away as I watched the vision of Emily Parker erased by the elevator door.

My loss, I thought to myself.

"Damn fucking right," I said to the doorman on my way out.

Chapter 99

I WAS STILL feeling no pain as I got home. There were streamers and a hallway full of balloons. An extra-large Carvel sheet cake was defrosting in the fridge. Seamus, master of ceremonies for MC's surprise bash, held court in the kitchen, directing the decorating and food prep.

"But, Grandpa, if this is a party, who's going to DJ?" Shawna said.

"Who do you think?" Seamus said, offended. "Sister Sheilah doesn't call me 'Father Two Turntables and a Microphone' for nothing, you know."

"What about the clown, Grandpa?" Chrissy, our baby, wanted to know. "And I don't see any balloon animals."

"It's on the list, child. Please, have ye no faith?" Seamus said, lifting his clipboard. "Now, Julia. How close are we with the pigs in a blanket?"

When everything was ready, I called upstairs to Mary Catherine's cell phone.

"Mary, I just got a call into work, and Seamus is nowhere to be found. Could you come down for emergency babysitting?"

"Give me five minutes, Mike," she said sadly.

She was there in three.

"Hello?" Mary Catherine said as she stepped slowly into the darkened apartment.

I hit the lights.

"Surprise!" we yelled.

Mary Catherine started crying as all the kids lined up and handed her their gifts with a hug. There were a lot of Starbucks cards and World's Best Teacher mugs. When Hallmark starts its World's Best Nanny line, we'll be the first customers. I thought MC was going to need resuscitation when Chrissy handed over her present: a homemade salt-dough doll of Chrissy herself.

"How old are you now?" I said when I caught Mary alone in the kitchen.

"That's a rude question to ask a lady," Mary Catherine said.

"Nineteen?" I guessed. "No, wait. Twenty-two?"

"I'm thirty, Mike. So there. Are you happy?"

I was genuinely surprised. MC looked like a college kid. So that explained it, her nuttiness. Turning thirty. Women didn't like that or something, right?

"Well, at least you're calling me Mike again instead of Mr. Bennett. I must have done something right. Saints preserve us."

I produced the gift I had gotten on the way home from Emily's hotel. Striemer Jewelers on 47th was actually closed when I arrived, but the owner, Marvin, who was working late, owed me a favor.

"If this is about our, eh, collision, all is forgiven, Mike," she said, staring at the small box. "I've already forgotten it."

"Open it."

She did. Inside was an amethyst pendant on a white gold chain, her birthstone.

"But," she said. "This is... How can we..."

"You tell me," I said into her ear as I put the necklace on her. "I don't know a damn thing about anything."

An aching expression of sadness was in Mary Catherine's face as her eyes went from the sparkling pendant to me.

"We'll talk after all that champagne wears off,

Mike," she said as she started to leave. I tried to grab her arm on the way out, but I missed, and she was gone. Second time tonight, I thought. Way to go, Mr. Smooth.

"Check me out!" Seamus yelled from the living room. I lifted my cake as the sound of an electric guitar started up. What now?

Seamus was standing in front of the TV. In his hands was the plastic guitar from the kids' Guitar Hero game. His eyes were closed, and he was biting his lip as he wailed the "Welcome to the Jungle" solo. I don't know what was louder, his Slash impression, the kids' shrieks of laughter, or my own.

"Well, what do you know?" I said, gleefully atomic-dropping down onto the couch in the middle of my guys for a front-row seat. "The clown showed up to the party after all."

Chapter 100

I WAS STILL catching up on Detective Division reports from the Mooney case two weeks later. Unfortunately, having my paperwork done for me had lasted exactly until the task force was disbanded.

The last and most aggravating detail of the case continued to stare at me, usually from the cover of a newspaper, morning after morning. What the hell had happened to Dan Hastings, the abducted Columbia kid?

I was banging out my fourth backed-up incident report of the morning when Chief Fleming came rap-rap-rapping at my office door. In her hand was the only perk of working at One Police Plaza, authentic takeout from neighboring Chinatown.

We ate in her much larger office. Outside her window, a big yellow sun shone brightly off the honking, unmoving Brooklyn Bridge traffic.

I scanned the East River for bodies floating among the garbage beneath the bridge as I worked my chopsticks. I believe in a working lunch.

The chief pointed at the *New York Post* on the desk behind her as we cracked fortune cookies.

"Seen the latest?" she said.

"Let me guess. 'Mike Bennett, slacker, still too dumb to locate missing Ivy Leaguer'?"

"It's not about you for a change. The first victim, Jacob Dunning—his father has created a charitable foundation in his kid's name."

I managed to roll my eyes and shake my head at the same time.

"Wow. Exactly what Mooney wanted," I said, chewing. "Exactly what Mooney was hoping for when he blew the poor kid's head off."

"I don't know, Mike. Isn't some good coming out of this thing better than the alternative?" she said. "What would you do with all that money?"

"I don't know," I said after a moment's reflection. I lifted a napkin and wiped orange sauce off my cheek.

"With my luck, I'll never have that kind of

problem. But I'll tell you one thing. I'd burn it before I'd do exactly what my kid's murderer wanted me to do."

"You're cold, Mike, you know that?" Carol said as her phone rang. She smiled and nodded as she lifted the receiver. "I like that in a cop.

"No shit!" she suddenly said. "Okay, okay. I'll send somebody by right away."

She looked dumbstruck as she racked her phone.

"Your ship just came in. Troopers picked up Dan Hastings along the turnpike in South Jersey. They took him home to his father's boat."

Chapter 101

I MET GORDON Hastings in the stateroom of his yacht, the *Teacup Tempest*, half an hour later. The Scottish media mogul was as sleek as a royal otter in his European-cut double-breasted suit. It was a far cry from the slept-in Margaritaville attire he was wearing at our first encounter.

Call me bitter, but staring at him, I couldn't forget his drunkenness, rudeness, and stupidity, and his trying to take a swing at me. Worst of all was the fact that Hastings's *New York Mirror* had led the NYPD smear job that had started three days after we took care of Mooney.

Accusations of overkill and police brutality were being lodged on a daily basis at Mooney's miraculous takedown. In fact, law enforcement use of .50 caliber ammunition had become the latest TV talking-head topic. How did that happen? I wondered.

"I want to apologize for how I acted," Hastings said in his Scottish accent. He gave me his best James Bond grin as he offered his hand. "It was unconscionable, inappropriate, and foolish."

"You couldn't be more correct," I told him, ignoring his hand as I went to talk to his son.

Dan Hastings was at the head of the enormous dining room table, scarfing down a plate of salmon, when I came in and closed the door. A mound of caviar in a sterling silver serving bowl waited by his elbow.

"I'm glad you made it back, son," I said, shaking the handicapped college kid's hand. "I'm Mike Bennett, the detective in charge of the Mooney case. I'd like to go over what happened to you."

"Well, the important thing is that the son of a bitch is dead, right?" Dan said with a weird smile.

"Yes, he certainly is," I said. "I just need to finish the paperwork. I need you to tell me what happened to you from the beginning."

Dan nodded as he hit a scoop of caviar. I noticed a slight tremble in his hand as he washed it down with some white wine.

"Let's see," he said, chewing. "I was coming out of the library and someone called me over by one of the campus buildings. The next thing I knew, I felt a blow at the back of my head. I woke up hours later in a cave of some sort. I never saw anyone. I was tied up, but after two weeks, I eventually got free. I told all this to the troopers."

"Humor me," I said with a grin. "How did you, um, how did you manage to survive for two weeks?"

There was a subtle hitch in his breath.

"There was food there," he said, avoiding my eyes. "After a week, I finally decided to try to crawl out."

"Wow, that's heroic," I said. "It must have been brutal."

I'm not sure whether Dan or the silverware jumped higher as I suddenly brought my fist down on the table. I sat down on the table right beside him.

"Maybe everybody else is willing to swallow your bullshit, son, but you obviously haven't looked into my eyes yet. I'm the person who has to clean up the messes other people leave behind. My only consolation is that I can smell lies from a very great distance.

"You're a terrible liar, Dan. That's not a bad thing. It's actually a virtue in my book. It means you're new to the world of being a bad person. But you need to stop lying to me. I won't put up with it."

He tried to look into my eyes but failed. He lowered his head toward his plate.

"It was Galina," he mumbled. "It was all Galina's idea."

I checked my notes. Galina Nesser was his Russian girlfriend. Christ, what a punk. Right out of the box, he throws his girlfriend under the bus.

"She and her uncle cooked up the whole scheme," he said. "It had nothing to do with the other kidnappings. They said we could piggyback it. What the hell you want from me, man? I'm handicapped!"

I scribbled in my pad, laid it down, stared at him.

"No, you're more like an insult to handicapped people," I said.

"What's five million dollars to a man like my father?" Dan said as he wept. "I just wanted to get away from him. You don't know what he's like. His guilt. I hate it. I hate him. I just wanted to get away. I just wanted to be alone."

That's where Dan was wrong. I did understand. I hated and wanted to get away from his father, too.

We could have charged Dan Hastings with a host of things—fraud, misleading an investigation. I decided to give him the worst punishment of all.

I grabbed the back of his wheelchair and pushed him back into the stateroom.

"Mr. Hastings, your son has something to tell you."

"What?" he said. "What is it, Dan?"

"I did it, Dad. I wasn't kidnapped. It was a trick. I took your money. It had nothing to do with that Mooney guy."

Gordon Hastings's regal face imploded like a demolished building. I guess he wasn't too jazzed about my smiling, told-you-so expression.

"I'm not pressing charges, Officer," he said, his shock replaced by the sneer that was his natural expression, "if that's what you were hoping for. I want you off this vessel."

"What a coincidence. I want me off this vessel, too. Even more than you," I said on my way out.

Chapter 102

GETTING INTO MY car in the Chelsea Piers marina parking lot, I still couldn't believe it. What was wrong with that kid? Setting up such complicated money transfers would have been impressive enough on its own. Dan had even convinced that crazy kid to platform-jump off a bridge in order to get him his money.

Wheelchair or no wheelchair, the kid was clever and charming and rich. Wasn't that enough? If he hated his father so much, why couldn't he muster up the guts and leave?

Dan must have liked all that money too much, I realized. Leaving would have been hard. Leaving would have required sacrificing luxury. Dan wanted to have his hate, yet not have to pay for it. Hate costs. Even Mooney could have told him that.

F. Scott Fitzgerald was wrong, I decided, looking at the shining yacht. The rich really were just like you and me. Just as stupid, petty, shortsighted, screwed-up, flawed. Just as human through and through.

Staring out at the yuppies doing their Tiger Woods impressions beside the boats, I thought of someone. I scrolled down through my speed-dial list until I found what I wanted and hit the Call button.

"VICAP. Parker speaking."

"Agent Parker," I said. "Bennett here. How are you?"

"Mike!" she yelled. She actually sounded happy to hear from me. She must have forgotten how we had said good-bye at her hotel.

"Hey, how are things up there? That party was fun. Man, was I trashed."

"Not more than me," I said. "Listen, I just found out we were right when we thought there was something funny about the Hastings kid's kidnapping. It turns out it was complete bullshit. The kid cooked it up with his Russian squeeze. They did it to rob his father. Nice, huh? Little early Father's Day present for the old man."

"Wow," she said. She was silent for a long beat.

"When Francis X. and I got into our shouting match, he said that today's youth was worthless. Sometimes I think maybe he was right. Maybe this world has lost its way."

I tried to say something then, but when I opened my mouth, no words came out. I only wanted what all parents want, a nice place for their kids to live in. It was scary and painful to think of all the crazy, bad things that could happen, the kind of bleak future that might await them.

I looked out at the water. Though the day was bright, the air whistling in through my cracked-open window was harsh, biting, frigid.

"I don't know about the world, Emily," I finally said. "All I know is that Mooney is dead, and we're still on the job."

I started the car and cranked up the heat.

"That might not exactly be happily ever after," I said, "but what the hell. It's a start."

About the Authors

James Patterson has had more *New York Times* bestsellers than any other writer, ever, according to *The Guinness Book of World Records.* Since his first novel won the Edgar Award in 1976, James Patterson's books have sold more than 170 million copies. He is the author of the Alex Cross novels, the most popular detective series of the past twenty-five years, including *Kiss the Girls* and *Along Came a Spider.* Mr. Patterson also writes the bestselling Women's Murder Club novels, set in San Francisco, and the top-selling New York detective series of all time, featuring Detective Michael Bennett.

James Patterson also writes books for young readers, including the award-winning Maximum Ride,

Daniel X, and Witch and Wizard series. In total, these books have spent more than 200 weeks on national bestseller lists, and all three series are in Hollywood development.

His lifelong passion for books and reading led James Patterson to launch a new website, ReadKiddoRead.com, to give adults an easy way to locate the very best books for kids. He writes full-time and lives in Florida with his family.

Michael Ledwidge is the author of *The Narrowback* and *Bad Connection,* and, most recently, the coauthor, with James Patterson, of *Run for Your Life.* He lives in New York City.

Books by James Patterson

FEATURING ALEX CROSS

I, Alex Cross
Alex Cross's Trial (with Richard DiLallo)
Cross Country
Double Cross
Cross
Mary, Mary
London Bridges
The Big Bad Wolf
Four Blind Mice
Violets Are Blue
Roses Are Red
Pop Goes the Weasel
Cat & Mouse
Jack & Jill
Kiss the Girls
Along Came a Spider

THE WOMEN'S MURDER CLUB

The 8th Confession (with Maxine Paetro)
7th Heaven (with Maxine Paetro)
The 6th Target (with Maxine Paetro)
The 5th Horseman (with Maxine Paetro)
4th of July (with Maxine Paetro)
3rd Degree (with Andrew Gross)
2nd Chance (with Andrew Gross)
1st to Die

FEATURING MICHAEL BENNETT

Worst Case (with Michael Ledwidge)
Run for Your Life (with Michael Ledwidge)
Step on a Crack (with Michael Ledwidge)

THE JAMES PATTERSON PAGETURNERS

Maximum Ride: The Manga 2 (with NaRae Lee)
Witch & Wizard (with Gabrielle Charbonnet)

Daniel X: Watch the Skies (with Ned Rust)
MAX: A Maximum Ride Novel
Maximum Ride: The Manga 1 (with NaRae Lee)
Daniel X: Alien Hunter (graphic novel; with Leopoldo Gout)
The Dangerous Days of Daniel X (with Michael Ledwidge)
The Final Warning: A Maximum Ride Novel
Maximum Ride: Saving the World and Other Extreme Sports
Maximum Ride: School's Out—Forever
Maximum Ride: The Angel Experiment

OTHER BOOKS

The Murder of King Tut (with Martin Dugard)
Swimsuit (with Maxine Paetro)
Against Medical Advice: One Family's Struggle with an Agonizing Medical Mystery (with Hal Friedman)
Sail (with Howard Roughan)
Sundays at Tiffany's (with Gabrielle Charbonnet)
You've Been Warned (with Howard Roughan)
The Quickie (with Michael Ledwidge)
Judge & Jury (with Andrew Gross)
Beach Road (with Peter de Jonge)
Lifeguard (with Andrew Gross)
Honeymoon (with Howard Roughan)
SantaKid
Sam's Letters to Jennifer
The Lake House
The Jester (with Andrew Gross)
The Beach House (with Peter de Jonge)
Suzanne's Diary for Nicholas
Cradle and All

When the Wind Blows
Miracle on the 17th Green (with Peter de Jonge)
Hide & Seek
The Midnight Club
Black Friday (originally published as *Black Market*)
See How They Run (originally published as *The Jericho Commandment*)
Season of the Machete
The Thomas Berryman Number

For previews of upcoming books by James Patterson
and more information about the author,
visit www.jamespatterson.com.

AMITYVILLE PUBLIC LIBRARY
3 5922 00255 7803